THIS
AGAIN?

BY ADAM BORBA

The Midnight Brigade
Outside Nowhere
This Again?

THIS AGAIN?

ADAM BORBA

Illustrations by Mercè López

LITTLE, BROWN AND COMPANY
New York Boston

Library of Congress Cataloging-in-Publication Data
Names: Borba, Adam, author.
Title: This again? / Adam Borba.
Description: First edition. | New York : Little, Brown and Company, 2024. | Audience: Ages 8–12. | Summary: Seventh grader Noah tries to avoid the worst day ever and help his future self win his eighth-grade class election using time travel.
Identifiers: LCCN 2023013552 | ISBN 9780316553186 (hardcover) | ISBN 9780316553391 (ebook)
Subjects: CYAC: Space and time—Fiction. | Elections—Fiction. | Student government—Fiction. | Middle schools—Fiction. | Schools—Fiction. | LCGFT: Novels.
Classification: LCC PZ7.1.B6695 Th 2024 | DDC [Fic]—dc23
LC record available at https://lccn.loc.gov/2023013552

ISBNs: 978-0-316-55318-6 (hardcover), 978-0-316-55339-1 (ebook)

JUN - - 2024
$16.99

Printed in the United States of America

LSC-C

Printing 1, 2024

For my fellow time travelers,
Erin, Charlie, and Hazy

PROLOGUE

NEXT THURSDAY...

Election Day

The sweat from Noah Nicholson's hands smeared the ink on his index cards. He shuffled the cards in his lap, trying to make sense of them. Only an hour ago, he'd had every word of his speech memorized. Now he couldn't recall his opening line if his life depended on it. And as far as he was concerned, it did.

Noah sat front and center in the first of two rows of chairs on his middle school auditorium's stage. He was in the seventh grade's 51st percentile for height, which he liked to lightheartedly boast made him above average. His brown hair was perfectly parted, and his button-up shirt had been dutifully ironed. Sadly, good hair and a crisp shirt are little help when you've completely forgotten what to say.

As usual, Noah was nervous. Normally when he was nervous, he talked and said whatever came to mind. But this afternoon, he couldn't leave anything to chance. Today needed to go *perfectly*. He was only one speech away from living up to his wildest expectations. One speech away from making all his hard work worth it. One speech away from turning the worst day of his life into the best.

If only he could remember how that speech was supposed to start.

In front of him, the school choir sang the fight song to a theater packed with his seventh-grade classmates. The song finished and the choir bowed to polite applause and filed into the stage's second row of chairs. The room vibrated with chatter. Hundreds of conversations overlapped, like a thousand seagulls at a beach. Noah's heart pounded. His head hurt. He took a deep breath and ran a hand over a wrinkle in his khakis. The wrinkle remained, as did his anxiety. His knees began to shake. Then Noah felt a hand on his shoulder and a gentle squeeze. His legs stopped bouncing and he turned to find Lucy Martinez sitting directly behind him. She wore her dark hair up and a sweater with a mockingbird knitted across the front. It was Noah's favorite sweater.

"Good luck," she said.

Noah pursed his lips and nodded.

"Vote for Noah!" called out someone in the crowd.

"Go Noah!" yelled another, followed by dozens of enthusiastic clappers, two hoots, and a holler.

Noah smiled weakly to the assembly. He was still adjusting to his newfound popularity.

At the podium, in a dusty blue suit and purple tie, Principal Thompson shook his head and tapped the microphone. "Quiet, please. The only campaigning that I should hear in this room will come from the candidates on this stage. Please be respectful to both nominees. They've each made tremendous efforts. This will be an honest and fair election."

Noah swallowed hard.

"Let's maintain our integrity," Principal Thompson continued. "If you're going to be unruly, we can cancel this assembly and everyone can go back to class." Someone coughed. A few chairs squeaked as students shifted uneasily. "Okay, then. Thank you to the show choir for another spirited performance." More polite applause from the room. Thompson gave a cordial nod to the choir and turned back to the microphone. "Without further ado, your first candidate to be next year's eighth-grade class president, Noah Nicholson."

The room erupted with cheers. Noah riffled through his

cards, smudging them further. He exhaled upon finding the beginning of his speech. He took another deep breath. He could do this. He *would* do this. His green eyes twinkled, and his lips curled into a smile. With confidence, Noah moved to take the podium.

But something was wrong. Noah felt...*stuck*. Like he was attached to his chair. Had something tugged the back of his pants? Feeling everyone watching and waiting, Noah tried again to stand. Even over the cheers he heard the rip—like a sheet of paper torn top to bottom. He sensed a draft below his belt loops.

He looked over his shoulder at Lucy, whose mouth hung open while the girl next to her giggled. Noah's face turned red. He tried to pull the tear in his pants together, but it was hopeless. In a panic, he spun to face Lucy, hiding the split in his khakis behind him. The room exploded with laughter. Noah felt a drop in his stomach and realized he was showing his underwear to the entire school.

He sprinted offstage.

But the damage was done.

1

LAST WEDNESDAY...

Eight and a Half Days Until the Election

Noah's room was a mess. The hamper in his closet had over-flowed and dirty clothes littered the carpet. His blanket lay twisted with a superhero sheet at the foot of his bed, next to an acoustic guitar. And a half dozen long-forgotten water glasses sat atop his bedside table and surrounded the shiny globe on his cluttered desk. A Harvard College pennant hung on the wall beside an autographed picture of bowling legend Four Fingers Finkelstein and a cluster of second- and third-place ribbons. In the midst of the chaos, Noah wrote on a large whiteboard. A wrinkle-free blue oxford shirt lay next to an unattended iron behind him, sizzling with steam. "I think I have it all figured out," he said. "Maybe."

Noah's nineteen-year-old brother stood in the doorway, holding a basket of folded laundry under his arm. "Oh yeah?" Paul was taller than Noah, and significantly more confident.

"Yeah." Noah nodded at his board. "A foolproof path to success in eight simple steps."

Paul stepped into the room to get a closer look at Noah's handiwork:

NOAH'S PLAN TO BECOME WILDLY HAPPY & SUCCESSFUL

1) Go undefeated in this year's bowling league tournament
2) Triumph at the presidential debate next Wednesday
3) Give an incredible speech at the assembly before the vote on Thursday
4) Be an amazing eighth-grade class president next year
5) Get elected president all four years of high school

6) Graduate at the top of my class
7) Go to Harvard
8) Teach physics at a university (one of
   the good ones)

Paul frowned. "I'd just worry about middle school, bud."

Noah put a cap on his felt marker. "Mom and Dad did all of this before they moved here to co-run the science department. And so did you. Well, except the last one. But you will, obviously. And I figure by the time I get to Harvard you'll have it all figured out, so it'll be a piece of cake for me."

Paul patted Noah on the back. "Sure, but I'm saying maybe focus on one thing at a time?"

Noah's lips curled. "I am. The list is in order."

Paul shook his head. "Right…Well, I love you, but my laundry is done and I have to drive all the way back to school."

Noah's shoulders slumped. "Already? Do you have time to drop me off? I was thinking you could give me some pointers for the debate and speech next week."

"Sorry. I've got finals coming and a class in a few hours that I haven't been to since before spring break. But I'll be home for the summer at the end of next week."

Noah scratched his head with the marker. "You haven't been going to class?"

Paul shrugged. "Attendance isn't mandatory. In college you kind of make your own priorities."

Noah stared in awe at his brother. College sounded amazing. Though not going to class didn't sound like Paul—the bulletin board in his bedroom held perfect attendance certificates from kindergarten through high school.

Paul wrapped a muscular arm around Noah and gave him a hug. "See you soon. I'll give you a call next week so we can talk through your election stuff. In the meantime, try not to take it so seriously. It's only middle school."

Noah watched his brother stroll toward the hall and run into his father at the threshold. The elbow patches on Dr. Nicholson's tweed sports coat were wearing thin. "Heading out?"

Paul shrugged. "Finals, Pop."

Dr. Nicholson nodded. "Well…study hard."

"Always, Pop." Paul gave his dad a pat on the back and squeezed past him down the hall with his laundry.

Dr. Nicholson looked sad to see his eldest go. Noah shared the feeling. Without Paul at home, all eyes would be on him, so Noah had to step up his game in seventh grade. He was now the sole object of his brilliant parents' attention. As if on cue, his dad turned his gaze to him. "Hey, bucko, hope we didn't wake you when we got home last night. Babysitter okay?"

Noah crossed his arms. He was pretty sure Paul had been left in charge of the house when he was twelve. But if he was going to be a good president, he should practice playing the part of the diplomat. "Don't you think I'm getting a little old for a sitter?"

"I do not. Your developing brain needs sleep and supervision. Speaking of which, I'd prefer that you didn't use an iron alone in your room."

Noah turned off the iron and unplugged it, even though he was positive that *Paul* had never been told he couldn't use one alone. "Just trying to look presentable, but I hear you. Did you have fun last night?"

Dr. Nicholson smiled. "You should have seen your mother. Paul and I thought she gave an incredible lecture.

Between us, I used to think proton magnetics was the most boring subject in the world. I mean, what is there to say that hasn't been said, right?"

Noah stared blankly.

His father didn't seem to notice. "But last night your mom had us all in the palm of her hand. She was a rock star presenting her new theory. I felt like we were giddy undergrads again. Honestly, thrilling is the only appropriate word to describe the night."

Noah nodded proudly. "That's fantastic, Dad." He'd given up on trying to wrap his head around proton magnetics ages ago. Instead, Noah focused his energy on finding other ways to impress his parents.

"It was, bucko. It was." Dr. Nicholson paused and patted a finger against his lips. "Noah, is it possible you used the blender to make a milkshake this morning?"

"Oh. Yeah…" A smile crept across Noah's face. That shake was delicious. He was close to perfecting his recipe. Paul had agreed. "You know how sometimes you need a sugar rush to get going in the morning? Big day today. I've got a game after school. Did I wake you?"

"No, I was working in the study. It's just that when I came into the kitchen, I discovered ice cream splattered all over the counter and the blender teetering on the edge. If I'd closed the door with any force that blender would have smashed to the floor. Can you please remember to clean up and put things away in the future?"

"Right. Sorry. Of course."

"Thank you." His father looked around the room and grimaced. "And bucko, do me a favor? Clean up in here, too. This place is a disaster. These dirty clothes are going to smell awful soon. Do your laundry, please."

Noah eyed his surroundings, surprised by the state of things. "Wow. Yeah. Not sure when all of this happened. I've just been so busy lately. School. The team. And especially my presidential campaign."

Noah anticipated that his father would be impressed, but instead Dr. Nicholson looked at his son with concern. "Do you think you're taking on too much? I'm worried about your grades, especially so close to the end of the school year. Your guidance counselor called."

Noah's eyes went wide. A bit of a surprise. He tried to give the appearance of shrugging it off. "The election will be over next week. I'll have plenty of time to catch up then."

"What if you win?"

Noah scratched his head. "I'll figure out how to deal with it next year. Paul did. And look at all the great things it started for him."

"You don't have to try to do *everything* your brother did."

"If only that were true...."

Dr. Nicholson wrinkled his nose. He opened his mouth to respond but stopped himself when the other Dr. Nicholson, Noah's mother, slipped into the room wearing a lab coat over her pants and blouse. She sipped a coffee. "Morning!"

"Congrats on last night, Mom. Heard you had the room riveted."

"Thanks, sweetie." She turned up her nose at the room. "You've got to clean this place. It'll turn into an unintended science experiment before you know it."

"Maybe tomorrow?"

His father sniffed and shook his head. "Maybe this morning."

Noah pulled on the oxford shirt and began buttoning. "I wish I could, but I have to get to school to start campaigning. Do you mind dropping me off a little early?"

"How's the campaign going, sweetie?"

Noah beamed and finished buttoning his shirt. "Slower than walking with Grandpa Joe to the park, but I've got a good feeling about today. I think I'm going to gain some real momentum." His parents didn't look so sure, but he was mostly trying to convince himself.

Like every weekday morning, the drop-off line in front of East Hills Middle School in Albany, New York, was backed up for blocks with buses, SUVs, and minivans.

Noah stood nervously next to a card table at the top of the school's steps while a river of students spilled into the brick building. He'd painted his slogan, *Know-A Good Thing When You See It! Vote for Noah*, in red on a sign tied to his table, and dozens of *Know-A Good Thing* campaign buttons sat on top. He held a button at arm's length offering it to anyone who passed. "Vote for me. Vote for me. Vote for Noah!" There were no takers, though several kids offered puzzled looks and one threw out a "Who's Noah?"

Across the steps, a blond girl with *Vote Claire* cupcakes was drawing a large crowd. Next to her, a boy manned a table with only a piece of spiral notebook paper taped to the front. The word *Gregg* was scrawled across the paper in pencil. You could barely see it. But you didn't need to. Gregg wore a white basketball jersey with green trim and exchanged pointed fingers and smiles with nearly every kid who entered the building. No one needed to ask who Gregg was.

Noah eyed his competition. How were they campaigning so effortlessly? And why did *he* find it so stressful? "Vote for Noah. Vote for Noah." The button remained in his outstretched hand.

A redheaded girl scowled at Noah's sign. "That's a terrible slogan."

Noah flinched. "It's clever."

"It looks like you don't know how to spell your name," the girl replied, and went inside.

Noah frowned at his sign and snuck another look at the mob of students grabbing cupcakes at Claire's table. "I should have baked brownies," Noah said woefully. Gregg's seemingly endless stream of "Morning," "Hey," and "Hello" persisted. Like always, everyone appeared genuinely excited to see Gregg. Noah wanted that.

"Hi, Gregg!"

Noah recognized the voice of Lucy Martinez. He turned as she climbed from her mother's silver sedan. His heart beat double time.

"Hi, Lucy!" Gregg responded. The school bell rang. Lucy opened her mom's rear door to grab something from the back seat. A handful of kids helped Claire pack her few remaining cupcakes and collapse her table and Gregg's. Gregg folded the piece of spiral notebook paper and slipped it into his pocket. Noah watched and sighed as the others wandered into school chatting happily.

He tossed his button onto the untouched pile and carefully unfastened and rolled up his sign.

"I'll take one."

Noah nearly jumped. He turned to find Lucy holding a pretzel-and-marshmallow model of the Empire State Building with both hands.

"A button, I mean," she continued. "If you can open the door for me." She nodded at the bulky model in her hands and then at the closed doors to the school.

"Really? Cool. Absolutely!" Noah grabbed a button and eyed a strap on her backpack. Should he pin it there? He thought better of it and gently placed the button on Fifth Avenue in front of the Empire State Building.

Lucy smiled. Noah stared at her model, impressed by the detail.

"Just missing the giant gorilla," he said.

"Oh?"

Noah's cheeks went red. "King Kong...Never mind."

She stared at her model.

Noah examined the ground. Was there a hole he could climb into? "I'm joking," he said. "You know, I've always felt the best jokes are the ones you have to explain are jokes in the first place."

"No, I understood," Lucy said. "I was just thinking the gorilla could have a tiny Principal Thompson in his hand. Missed opportunity."

She smiled at him. He smiled back.

"Could you, um?" She gestured toward the doors.

"Ah! Totally. Sorry!" Noah hurried to the entrance and pulled a handle. He pointed at his button on Fifth Avenue. "You know, that doesn't mean you have to vote for me." Noah cringed. "I don't know why I said that. Of course you know."

Lucy nodded. "Thanks for getting the door, Noah."

He watched her walk down the hall to her homeroom. "You're welcome," he called, and cringed again. He peeked at his watch and his eyes bulged. He hurried back to his things and quickly tossed his buttons into a cardboard box, folded the table, snatched his sign, and ran to the door. Hands full, he groaned and looked around. Noah was alone.

He leaned the table against one door, pulled open another and awkwardly propped it with a foot, grabbed the table, and rushed inside.

2

CRUNCHING NUMBERS...

Eight and a Quarter Days Until the Election

"The polls look awful," Samar said. "You should quit."

Noah combed his hair in the boys' restroom's cracked mirror. "What do you mean polls? The school doesn't do polls."

"I asked everyone in my homeroom. Jenny Fitzman is the only person voting for you. That's one out of thirty."

"Well, two out of thirty," Noah said. "Jenny and you."

"Technically I'm still undecided."

Noah watched Samar pull a tie from his backpack and

put it on. Samar was short and skinny, and used entirely too much hair spray, so his hair never moved. He was also unapologetically direct with his friends. "I'll never understand why you choose to be so ambitious even though absolutely everything gives you anxiety."

Noah shrugged. "People are complicated and I'm a person."

"A person who is delusional if he thinks he has a chance to be class president," Samar said.

Noah sighed.

A toilet flushed and Darnell Armstrong stepped from a stall. He was stout with a shaved head, and didn't have a problem pairing socks, sandals, and skinny jeans. "Only me, Mohsen Azimi, and Susan Bloomer are voting for you in my homeroom...so, maybe you *should* quit?" Darnell had a talent for making most everything sound like a question. He washed his hands while Noah exhaled.

"I can't let down everyone who nominated me," Noah said.

"We nominated you because you asked us to," Samar said. "You're going to come in dead last."

"Dead last?" Noah asked.

"Behind write-in votes for that new lunch lady who rides the moped to school," Samar said.

"It's a sweet moped," Darnell said.

"Super sweet," Samar said.

Noah turned out his palms optimistically. "Being eighth-grade class president is a family tradition. And a lot can happen in a week."

Samar nodded. "Absolutely it can. Jenny's vote for you didn't feel all that firm."

"It's great having you guys to support me," Noah said.

"If you embarrass yourself in front of the whole school, it'll look bad on all of us," Samar said.

"Thanks," Noah said.

"No problem," Darnell and Samar replied.

Noah hung his head.

"You know we're just looking out for you, right?" asked Darnell.

Noah nodded.

"Good." Darnell grabbed a paper towel and dried his hands. "By the way, why'd you take the bus this morning?"

Noah frowned. "The bus? I got a ride from my dad."

Darnell frowned harder. "I saw you at the bus stop in front of the Delancey Street Mini-Mart. Weren't you eating one of those coconut, honey, and marshmallow candy bars that you like?"

Noah shook his head. "That wasn't me."

"But didn't you wave?" Darnell asked. "And aren't you the only person in town who eats those?"

"Yeah, they're gross," Samar said.

"First off, they're not gross," Noah said. "They're an acquired taste. And second, I don't know what to tell you. I wasn't at the Mini-Mart this morning."

Darnell furrowed his brow. "If you say so?"

Noah eyed Samar. "Why did you put on a tie?"

Samar adjusted his knot in the mirror. "I read a study that found people are three percent less likely to say no to someone wearing a tie, and I need to ask Ms. Tucker if I can do extra credit for Pre-Algebra. I just know I tanked that test yesterday."

"You probably got an A-minus," Noah said.

Samar deflated. "Exactly."

"Well," Noah said, "it looks nice."

Samar smiled, and the boys charged out of the restroom into their school's crowded, sticky linoleum halls where **GO LEPRECHAUNS!** and **DON'T FORGET YOUR TIX TO THE SPRING FLING** banners hung from the ceiling. Noah pulled a math book from his faded green locker and took a step back when the basketball team bumped shoulders against him and his friends. "Watch it, geeks," said the tallest one. Noah admired the team floating down the hall wearing their game jerseys over T-shirts, trading high fives with each other. Six years earlier, his older brother had been one of those popular kids. How had Paul made it look so easy? Was it because he was taller? Noah rolled his shoulders back and lifted his chin.

Darnell rubbed his arm. "Isn't it funny how they always manage to knock into us?"

"If I didn't know better, I'd say they were doing it on purpose," Samar said.

Noah closed his locker. "It's just a little hazing, guys. It means they like us."

"No, we don't, geek," called the player at the back of the pack.

Noah lowered his voice. "Well, at least it means they're on a path to like us. They know who we are and that's the first step."

"I've gone to school with all of those guys since kindergarten and I doubt half of them could tell you my name," Samar said.

"I should have signed up for basketball in fifth grade instead of tennis," Noah said.

"Yep, that's the thing that's been holding you back," Samar joked.

"I'm serious," Noah said.

"You don't even like basketball," Samar said.

Noah shrugged. "But *they* do. And besides, I might've been a natural."

"If you had a natural ability to play basketball in the fifth grade, wouldn't you still have it?" Darnell asked.

"Now we'll never know," Noah said.

A picture of a striped kitten that read NUMBERS DON'T LIE, BUT MY CAT DOES hung above Ms. Tucker's desk in Pre-Algebra. Ms. Tucker's long dark hair had streaks of bright purple. She paired her skirts with T-shirts of bands Noah recognized from posters in Paul's college dormitory. She'd been a gymnast before dedicating her life to teaching math to preteens. The kids in her classes either had crushes on her or wanted to be her. She was half the age of most of the faculty at East Hills, and once upon a time, she'd been a student there, too.

Noah watched hopefully from his seat while Ms. Tucker gracefully navigated herself between desks delivering graded exams. Noah's test was placed in front of him, and his face fell.

"I think you made a mistake, Ms. Tucker. There's no way I got a sixty-five."

"Actually, I gave you an extra five points for showing your work so clearly. It's fascinating how you arrived at some of your answers. Just bafflingly wrong, Noah. But your drawing of that stick figure offering me balloons and a puppy if I gave you a good grade made me laugh."

"You think a sixty-five is a good grade?" Noah asked.

"Better than a sixty," she said.

"But not quite a seventy." Noah's heart pounded. "Could I have gotten a seventy if I'd used colored pencils? Brightened up those numbers with some pizzazz? What do you need from me, Ms. Tucker? I'm trying here and your class is going to sink my GPA. Samar and Darnell are going to leave me in the dust. Is a seventy really too much to ask?"

Lucy Martinez chuckled at her desk. Noah glanced at her across the room, pleasantly surprised by her recent string of attention.

Ms. Tucker shook her head. "You could have gotten a seventy if you'd answered more questions correctly, but you're funny. And my door is always open after school if you need a little extra help." She placed the final test in front of Samar. "Nice job, Samar. You nearly edged out Darnell for the best grade in the class. And nice tie, too."

Samar grinned at his score of ninety-seven and straightened his tie. Darnell held up his ninety-eight and exchanged a salute with his friend.

"Nerds," coughed Gregg's friend Perry, also from the basketball team. Half the room giggled.

Ms. Tucker rolled her eyes. "That's not how we talk to each other in this class. And I would hope it's not how we talk to each other outside of this class either."

"Oh, trust me, Ms. Tucker," Perry said, "I'd never talk to those guys outside of class."

"Good one, Perry," Samar said. "But don't let our massive intellects intimidate you."

"And don't be scared of my athletic ability," Perry said.

"Don't you know the three of us are co-captains of the bowling team?" Darnell asked.

Noah's eyes went wide.

"We don't have a bowling team," Gregg said.

Noah gestured to his friends to stop talking. Why didn't they understand that bowling wasn't cool at East Hills?

"It's a club team," Samar boasted, either not noticing or not caring about Noah's signals. "Through the *library*."

Lucy laughed again. Noah slid low in his chair. Could he hide under his desk? The bell rang before he could try, and most of the class bolted for the door.

Noah shook his head at Samar and Darnell.

"Just because basketball is more fashionable than bowling with our peer group doesn't mean Gregg and Perry should be considered superior athletes," Samar said. "I'd like to see them bowl a turkey like you did last week. Give yourself some credit, Noah."

"Yeah," Darnell said. "Bowl three strikes in a row with their height and center of gravity? Highly unlikely, right?"

Noah sighed, then smiled when he noticed Lucy grinning at him as she left the room. He turned to Samar and Darnell. "Did you guys see that?"

"See what?" Samar asked.

"Noah, can I talk to you a moment?" Ms. Tucker asked from her desk.

"Never mind," Noah mumbled to his friends. "See you next period."

Samar and Darnell waved goodbye. Noah grabbed his bag and slunk over to Ms. Tucker. "Hi."

"I'm circling back on my offer to help you after school. You're right about your GPA. Honestly, you're barely holding on in this class and if you don't get at least a B on your next exam, I'm not sure you're going to be able to stay in the honors program next year."

Noah blinked. "But I have to stay in honors. Darnell and Samar are in honors. And if I'm not in honors next year, I won't be on a path to get into Harvard. And if I don't go to Harvard...I mean, if I don't go to Harvard for undergrad, how will I ever get my master's there? Or my doctorate? Or my *second* doctorate? You know who my parents are, right, Ms. Tucker? And my brother? Paul was one of your students. Wait. Are you saying my entire life depends on whether or not I get a B on the next exam?" Noah began to hyperventilate. "Do you mind if I sit down?" He sat on the floor.

Ms. Tucker's head snapped back. "Whoa. Noah, take it easy. I'm not saying that at all. In fact, for absolute clarity, I'm saying the exact opposite. Your life does *not* depend on this next exam. Do you hear me?"

Noah stared at the gray tiled floor and felt the classroom spin.

Ms. Tucker gave a gentle wave from her desk. "If you're not in honors classes with your friends next year it won't be the end of the world. It might even be good for you. You'll have time to focus on your work at your own pace and catch up, and you won't have to compete with them."

Noah held his head in his hands. "But I've *always* competed with them."

"Yes. That's my point. I worry you're putting a lot of unnecessary and unfair pressure on yourself by making comparisons to your friends and your family. There's a decent chance your grades would improve if you didn't. You just need to be Noah. But if it's important to you to stay in the honors program next year, there's a way to do it. And that's to study and get a better grade on your final test. Maybe focus on this class instead of your presidential campaign?"

Well, at least she knew he was running. Could teachers vote, he wondered? "My brother Paul was president, so I have to be president. And I need to win the election to get into Harvard."

"Noah. You don't. Colleges don't care what you did in middle school."

"Well, technically, Ms. Tucker. But if I want to be class president my senior year of high school, I'm going to have to be president of the eighth grade first."

"That's completely not the case. A lot of things will happen to you over the next few years. Some of it will be important, and some of it won't. At all. You just have to decide where you'd like to spend your energy."

"I want to do everything."

"You can't, Noah. No one can."

"My brother did, so we're going to have to agree to disagree." Noah put on a brave face and picked himself up off the floor.

"I'm serious, Noah. College is a long way away and this election seems to be taking up a big portion of your time recently."

"And it's time well spent. Trust me, I can win the election *and* ace the next exam."

"And trust *me*, in the grand scheme of things, you'll be fine regardless of whether you win or lose. So, again, I'll be here this afternoon if you need a little extra help."

"Thanks," Noah said, heading to the door. "But I have something incredibly important after school."

3

HAVING A BALL...

Eight Days Until the Election

Bowl-O-Rama's fifteen lanes were packed. They always were on Wednesday afternoons for league play. Neon lightning bolts and swirls flashed on the walls, and the sounds of a constant barrage of rolling balls and falling pins echoed across the building.

Noah's body lurched forward, and he launched a bowling ball down a lane. The ball rolled until it sent a pin careening into nine others for a flawless strike. *Clink!* He pumped his fist in the air. "I am the greatest twelve-year-old athlete alive!"

"Nice," Samar said. He ran his fingers over the air dryer on the ball-return machine. "That's three strikes in a row! I can't believe you bowled turkeys in back-to-back weeks."

"Can you believe that puts us down by only two?" Darnell said from the score table. He sat next to a middle-aged lady in a *Sub Shack* T-shirt. An old man and a twenty-something woman with a mohawk lounged on the bench behind them, also wearing shirts from the sandwich shop.

"You kids are getting lucky," the old man whined.

"Luck has nothing to do with it, Bernard," Samar said. "We've been training rigorously for months."

Noah grabbed a hand towel off the bench on the boys' side of the lane and dried his face. "I think I can get another strike."

"But we only need three pins to win or two to tie," Samar said. "Just roll a ball down the middle of the lane and let's lock this up. If we win, we skip the first two rounds of the playoffs on Tuesday and go straight to the finals."

"The right side of the lane is rolling so smoothly this afternoon," Noah said. "I'm locked in and only eight pins away from a new personal record. I can bowl another strike."

"Kid," the old man said, "don't be ridiculous. Nobody can bowl four strikes in a row. That's why there isn't a name for it."

"It's called a hambone," Samar said.

The young woman with the mohawk looked up. "Really?"

Noah nodded. "Yep. Or a four-bagger."

The old man rolled his eyes. "Oh, baloney! It doesn't matter what it's called. You can't do it, so just take the win. Can't have it all, kid."

Noah shook his head. "Oh yeah? Watch me." He grabbed his ball from the return machine while the pins finished resetting.

"Noah, don't," Samar said. "Please. We just need a few points."

Darnell wiped sweat from his brow. "Yeah, maybe play it safe? Roll one right down the middle?"

"Listen to your friends," suggested the mohawked woman.

Noah stared down his competition and stepped to the lane. He lifted his ball and lined up behind the lane's middle arrow.

"You can try to beat your record next season," the old man called.

Noah narrowed his eyes at the triangle of standing pins, begging to be knocked over. Why take the easy win when you can have the harder one? Noah glanced over his shoulder and took a step to the right.

"Don't do it," Samar warned.

But how could he turn his back on perfection? Noah

stared down the lane, pulled his arm back, and let the bowling ball fly. The ball rolled up the right side of the lane and curved toward the front pin. Noah held his breath. Another perfect strike coming…Ten feet away from the pins. Five feet. Noah bit his lip, and the ball's rotation took a sudden backspin, turned sharply to the right, and went off the lane.

Gutter ball!

Ten pins left standing.

Noah's face fell. Darnell and Samar covered theirs. The world spun. Noah's mouth was dry, and his heart pounded. Woozy, he stepped back and dropped to a knee.

"Game over, kid," the old man called.

"Good luck in the first round of the tournament," the middle-aged woman said to Darnell. "Maybe we'll see you in the finals." She patted him on the back, exchanged handshakes, and walked off with her team.

Noah closed his eyes until the nausea passed. He opened them and stared at the untouched pins at the end of the lane. He had tried for everything and ended with nothing. Maybe there was a lesson to be learned? Noah climbed to his feet and sheepishly turned to his friends. "Sorry, guys. I really thought I could do it."

"Well, on the bright side, we still made the playoffs, right?" Darnell said.

"Tuesday is gonna be tough," Samar said. "The Senior

Center is extremely competitive this year. Mr. Malusky from Eddie's Hardware retired so he's playing for them now."

"How is that fair?" Darnell asked.

"He and his wife moved into the retirement community," Samar said. "It would be unfair if he still bowled for Eddie's."

Darnell scratched an ear. "I guess?"

Noah dug out his wallet to make amends. "You guys want more lemonade?"

"No thanks," Darnell said. "I've already had a couple glasses and if I have too much sugar in the afternoon...I don't know, I might have trouble sleeping?"

"Same here," Samar said.

Noah exhaled. "We'll beat them in the finals." He shook his head and made his way across the busy alley to the concession stand for more lemonade for himself.

"Right with you," the man behind the counter said, and disappeared into the kitchen.

Noah took a seat on a stool and waited for him to return. He heard fingernails drumming at the end of the counter and looked over to find Lucy standing there with a smile. His lips parted. What was she doing here?

"Hi," she said.

"You bowl?"

"I just come here to rent shoes."

Noah glanced at the dusty pair of red-and-tan leather bowling shoes on his feet and the clean white tennis shoes on hers. He laughed at her joke. "It's a shame shoes are the only thing they let you rent at bowling alleys. Can you imagine bowling pants?"

"Sounds itchy. Hats?"

Noah nodded. "Like a fedora?"

"Sure! Or maybe a burlap sack tied around your forehead with a shoelace?"

Noah laughed. "I'd worry that might throw off my balance."

Lucy shrugged. "Sometimes you have to make compromises for fashion. I was wondering if you'd be here."

Noah got goosebumps. "You were?"

"Yeah," she said like it was no big deal. "Because you guys were talking about bowling in class?"

"Right...I've never seen you at the alley before."

"Bowling isn't my thing."

Noah deflated. "Oh."

Lucy bit her lip and backpedaled. "Not that there's anything wrong with bowling. I haven't really tried it since I was...five? I'm here with my little brother. He likes the arcade." She pointed at a room with blinking lights, race car sounds, and a steady stream of clinking quarters, explosions, and groans.

"It's a good arcade," he said.

She nodded. "That's what I hear, but I never got into video games either."

"You should give bowling another shot. It's fun."

Lucy glanced at the lanes and the roomful of smiles. She smiled, too, then frowned. "I don't think any of my friends would be into it."

"Maybe we could bowl together?"

She smirked. "You want to go bowling with me?"

Noah turned red. "What? No. I mean, it wouldn't be like we were bowling together." His eyes drifted around the alley. "Just, maybe, next to each other in the same lane…taking turns? Unless you'd, um…It doesn't have to be…like, official. But if you wan—"

Suddenly, Noah's jaw dropped and he fell silent. Lucy's head tilted and she waited for him to continue, but Noah forgot he'd been speaking. All he could do was stare at a boy on the other side of the alley.

A boy who looked *identical* to him.

It was like looking into a mirror—except the boy was leaning against the exit and wearing a different shirt. A navy shirt with light blue *X*'s across the middle. Noah had the same one in his closet. His heart pounded. "How?"

Lucy frowned at Noah and turned to see what he was staring at.

But the double was gone.

She looked back at Noah. "Are you okay?"

"Can you excuse me a minute? I think I'm losing my mind."

Noah sprinted across the bowling alley before she could respond, dodging folks renting shoes and waiting for lanes to open. He frantically looked left and right, even down under benches. But there was no sign of the double.

Noah flung open the exit door into the parking lot. Not a soul in sight other than the middle-aged woman from Sub

Shack climbing into an old red minivan. "Nice rolling today, kid. Tough luck at the end."

Noah nodded at the woman, breathed heavily, and scanned the lot. Across the street, a city bus pulled away. A small hand emerged from one of the bus's tinted windows and gave a wave.

Stunned, Noah raised a hand and waved back.

4

A VISITOR...

The Nicholsons' dining room was decorated with Noah's parents' framed degrees from Harvard, shelves of mathematics and physics books, and photographs of Paul winning awards, giving his valedictorian speech, and sitting in his freshman dorm. There were also two pictures of Noah— one of Noah on a tricycle, and the other of him playing the guitar at a lake. The center of the dining table was covered with porcelain figurines of characters from classic books that Noah's grandmother had been gifting the family every

Christmas for nearly twenty years (they weren't sure where else to keep them).

Noah hadn't said much at dinner while his parents recapped his mother's triumphant lecture. His folks' plates were nearly empty, but his was still piled high with something tan and slimy with chunks of pink. The Nicholsons had recently instituted what they called Gourmet May, attempting new recipes each evening to break the endless stream of takeout and delivery. While Noah's folks were spectacular at cracking the mysteries of the cosmos, cooking a decent hamburger or grilled cheese was beyond their capabilities. May had been a rocky month in the Nicholson home.

Noah stared at a figurine of Alice in Wonderland meeting Tweedledee and Tweedledum. *Twins.* He'd never given the little ceramic sculpture much thought, but now it made his skin crawl. Could he actually have a twin of his own running around town and popping into bowling alleys? It had been a while since Noah had blinked. His parents eyed him with concern.

"Do you not like the salmon casserole?" his mother asked.

Noah flinched. He forced a smile and peered up. "No, it's great. Sorry, I guess I'm not hungry."

His parents exchanged looks.

"Something on your mind?" his father asked.

Noah sized up his parents. How much could he reveal without sounding delusional? "Do you think somewhere out in the world there could be a person who looks exactly like you?"

"Scientifically speaking anything is possible, bucko," his father said.

"But I mean *identical*," Noah said. "Is that possible?"

"Well, it's astronomically unlikely," his mother said. "But your father and I know as much as anyone that as soon as you say something can't happen, the universe finds a way to present evidence you're wrong."

Noah's father chuckled. "And unfortunately, the universe usually shares that evidence with some scientist you didn't get along with in grad school who'll publish their findings and make you look like a knucklehead."

Noah slouched in his seat.

His mother reached across the table and put a hand on his. "But no one can be *exactly* like you, sweetie. Your heart, your intelligence, your sense of humor? That's the stuff that makes you, *you*." She gave him a smile. "You're one of a kind."

Noah nodded and wished his mother's words made him feel better.

After dinner, Noah navigated the mess on his bedroom floor, sat on his bed, and played his guitar. Usually it took his mind off things, but today hadn't been usual. Noah strummed and riffed out some notes—and sounded good—but his heart wasn't in it that evening. He put the guitar aside, untangled his sheets and tucked himself into bed. Unfortunately, he could only toss and turn and worry.

He stared at the ceiling for hours replaying the events from the bowling alley. He'd acted for himself and not for his team, and they'd all lost. Now they'd have to try to advance the hard way through the tournament. Ugh. He twisted beneath the covers.

He replayed his last conversation with Lucy. She had a great laugh. And seemed genuinely glad to see him. She wasn't technically in the popular crowd, but that was only because she was friendly to everyone. Maybe she was just being nice to him, too? Why couldn't he have admitted he wanted to go bowling with her? If he had, he wouldn't have noticed his stupid look-alike and sprinted away from her, mid-conversation. A fresh wave of embarrassment washed over him. Noah kicked off his blanket and rolled to his side.

Then his thoughts drifted to his grades. Maybe Ms. Tucker was right, and he should spend more time studying. But based on his last test, how could he possibly get a B on his next exam? Paul never had to work this hard! Math had always been a challenge for Noah, but Pre-Algebra was impossible. What would life be like if he wasn't in honors classes with Darnell and Samar for eighth grade? He'd be alone.

But the thing that kept him tossing and turning the most was the double. It was so eerie to stare into his own eyes and know they *weren't his eyes*. Who was that boy?

Then Noah remembered the double's blue shirt. His aunt Maureen had bought it for him as a gift on a vacation she took to London. It wasn't the most common shirt on the planet. He'd never seen another like it. Noah eyed his closet door. And worried.

He stared harder at the door, attempting to see through it. But X-ray vision remained another ability he lacked.

He climbed from bed and tiptoed to the closet. Noah pulled open the door and gasped.

Hanging in the nearly empty closet was the blue shirt. He stepped over a pile of dirty clothes on the floor and rubbed the fabric between his fingers to prove it was really there.

Tap-tap-tap.

Noah jumped and turned to his window.

Tap-tap.

He let go of the shirt and felt his muscles tense.

Tap.

Noah took a deep breath and crept toward the sound. Through the glass, beneath the night sky, a silhouette stood in the shadow of the apple tree that grew outside his ground floor bedroom.

The figure gave another tap on the glass.

Noah bit his lip and lifted the window.

On the opposite side of the windowsill, his double bit into a coconut, honey, and marshmallow candy bar. He wore the blue shirt from the closet and a backpack that looked like the one hanging from Noah's desk chair.

Noah held a hand to his chest. "Who are you?"

"I'm you from the future. And I'm here to make sure you're elected eighth-grade class president."

Noah's jaw dropped and he froze.

"You should close your mouth," the double said. "We look smarter that way."

Noah's heart felt like it was pounding out of his chest, and he was having trouble forming complete thoughts. How on earth was he supposed to close his mouth after hearing something like that?

He put a hand beneath his chin and pushed his jaw shut. He stared. "Me? From the…future?"

"That's right."

Noah braced himself against the window frame to keep from toppling over. "But…that's impossible."

"It is for you right now," the double said. "But I assure you that next week it'll be very, very possible."

Noah shook his head. "The pressure finally got to me. I'm having a nervous breakdown."

The double rolled his eyes. "I promise you're not. This is totally real."

"But it can't be." Noah wiped his eyes and stuck his head out the window to get a closer look at the other boy. A perfect twin. Identical. Their faces less than a yard apart. *How?*

Noah squinted, but the boy remained. He couldn't believe his eyes. Or his ears. "How do I know you are who you say you are?"

The double thought for a moment. "You were the one who accidentally broke Grandma Helen's vase at Thanksgiving last year, you don't have a clue how to divide fractions, you hated the new salmon casserole recipe this evening, and you've had a crush on Lucy Martinez since the second grade when she gave her report on the phases of the moon for Science and you realized she was one of the smartest kids in our class."

"Whoa."

"Sorry about disappearing at the bowling alley. I thought I might be able to catch you before Darnell and Samar got up from the lane, but I couldn't have Lucy spot me, too." The double took a final bite from the candy bar and raised the purple wrapper to the window. "Mind throwing this away?"

Noah took the wrapper, amazed. "You like Coconut Chaos bars, too?"

The double cocked his head. "Of course I do. They're delicious. They're just an acquired taste. Also, I'm you, Noah. Keep up."

Noah tossed the wrapper into a trash can next to his desk and poked his head back out the window. There was still a 95 percent chance he was hallucinating, but he was curious as to how a future version of himself had ended up outside his house. "So what are you doing here?"

The double crossed his arms and lowered his voice. "We better go for a walk so we don't wake Mom and Dad."

"Because they don't know about you?"

"Obviously. And they won't until they invent time travel next week."

Noah blinked. "Mom and Dad are going to inven—"

"*Yes*. Come on, it's chilly."

Caught up in the excitement, Noah hadn't realized how cold he was in front of the open window. He hugged his arms to his chest. "Let me grab a jacket."

45

"Can you bring me the gray sweatshirt?"

Noah shook his head, disappointed with himself. "I lost it."

"It's between the bed and the bedside table. You were going to find it this weekend."

"Huh. Thanks." Noah's lips curled.

"Welcome. Hurry up, I'm cold."

5

BRIGHT FUTURE...

One Week and One Night Until the Election

Noah grabbed a jacket from his closet and slipped it on over his pajamas. Then he tied on a pair of tennis shoes and carefully moved his water glass–covered bedside table. A gray sweatshirt lay smushed between the furniture. "He was right," Noah mumbled to himself.

He picked up the sweatshirt and stepped to the window. Noah frowned into the darkness of the unknown.

The double sighed and seemed to read his mind. "Come on, if you can't trust yourself, who can you trust?"

Noah shrugged. Hard to argue with that. He climbed out the window and the double helped him down.

"Thanks again," Noah said. He handed off the sweatshirt. "I thought I lost that for good."

"Shhh." The double pulled on the sweatshirt and gestured away from the house.

The boys strolled down the tree-lined sidewalk, hands in pockets, and identical blue sneakers on their feet. It took Noah a moment to realize they seemed identical because they actually were the same shoes—only the double's pair must have been slightly older.

A million questions raced through Noah's mind while he examined the double. It was so strange to be looking at himself. It felt like a dream. He reached out a finger and touched the double's arm.

"Please don't poke me."

"Sorry. Just wanted to see if you were real."

The double sighed. "I get it. This is a lot for you."

"Yeah…" Noah pulled his eyes from the double and looked down at the pavement. "Where are we going?"

"I was thinking we could circle the block."

Noah glanced around his neighborhood. It was late, so there wasn't a single light on in any of the houses. It was nice being on his street when everything was so peaceful. Hopefully they wouldn't trip on anything in the dark.

The double pulled a flashlight from his pocket and clicked it on.

Noah eyed the beam, impressed. "You carry a flashlight?"

"I planned ahead. And that's what I'm going to help you do."

Noah nodded and tapped his chin. "What do I call you?"

"Well, I'm Noah, too, obviously. But if it helps you to give me a different name, maybe you can call me Future?"

"That's kind of cool."

"I know. Also, for the record, technically I'm from the present and you're from the past, but I understand that's a lot for you to wrap your head around. Also, Present isn't as good of a name. It would just sound like we were taking attendance."

Noah tried to process what Future was saying and nodded. "Yeah, let's stick with Future."

"Sounds good."

"I can't believe Mom and Dad are going to figure out how to time travel. That's incredible. I didn't even know they were working on that."

"They're not yet. But on Friday night they'll go out and buy a new blender that'll inspire them. And once they wrap their heads around a couple core concepts, they knock out their time machine in a few hours."

"They're inspired by a blender?"

"It has a reverse function. That's a revolution in blending. But it's not about the button on the blender. It's that the blender sparks a big realization. Mom called it an epiphany."

"Wow."

"Yep."

Noah eyed the straps over Future's shoulders. "What's in the backpack?"

"Just some shirts, socks, and stuff. I know you haven't done laundry for a while."

"You really do plan ahead."

Future snapped his fingers and pointed at Noah. "Now you're getting it."

"How far ahead in the future are you from?"

"Eight and a half days."

"So, like, right after the election?"

"Pretty much."

"Do I have a chance to win?"

"With my help."

Noah smiled and let it fade. "Are you sure? Honestly, I don't know if my campaign is going very well. It's almost like the whole election is a popularity contest."

"Noah, it *is* a popularity contest. And your campaign is going horribly. But if you listen to me, you're going to become the most popular kid in school by the end of next week."

"How?"

"I've been there before. You know how tests are easy when you know the answers?"

"Sure."

Future draped an arm over Noah's shoulder. "Well, I have all the answers to your life."

Noah and Future stood on the sidewalk in front of their neighbors' house. With all the new information tumbling around in his brain, Noah was exhausted and finally ready for bed, but he didn't want to be rude. Especially to himself. "So where are you going to sleep tonight?"

Future eyed their open window. "I thought I could crash in our room."

"What about Mom and Dad?"

"Well, the closet is pretty big."

Noah frowned. "You want to sleep in the closet?"

"Actually, I was thinking you could sleep in the closet."

"Me?" Noah shook his head. "No way. It's my bed."

"*Our* bed. Plus, I'm a guest and almost two weeks older than you. Respect the seniority."

"It's my bed. Your bed exists after the election."

Future groaned. "Maybe we trade off on who sleeps in the closet?"

"Trade off? How long are you planning on staying?"

"I can't leave until Mom and Dad invent time travel. Their time machine doesn't come on the journey with the traveler, so I'm stuck here until they build it."

Noah processed the implications. "That doesn't sound ideal."

"It's a new technology. Mom and Dad haven't had time to iron out the kinks."

"But they let you use it anyway?"

Future shrugged. "Well, yeah. As one of their initial

tests. It's not that far back. And I'm going to fix our life, so it's for a good cause."

"What's it like?"

"Traveling through time?" Future gazed at the stars. "It's instant. One moment you're sitting on the time machine and the next you drop to the floor and the machine is gone. Maybe a few things moved around the living room, but that's kind of it. It's just a different day on the calendar. In my head I've been calling it my day shift. Like I shifted the days around and it's my job?"

Noah nodded. "I like that."

"Thanks. Me too."

Noah admired Future. "I still can't get over how weird it is looking at myself like this."

Future sighed. "Well, hurry up and get used to it. You're going to have to be completely focused for this to work. I'll be giving you a lot of detailed instructions and you'll need to follow them to the T. But if you do, everyone at school will be calling you Mr. President next year."

"Really? You think everyone will call me Mr. President? That sounds kind of goofy."

Future tossed his hands in the air. "Not literally. But you know what I mean. Just do exactly what I say no matter how ridiculous it seems, and you'll get everything you want. Can you do that?"

Noah raised his chin. "Absolutely."

"Do you promise?"

Noah smiled. "I promise."

"Great," said Future. "Sleep in the closet tonight, I'm taking the bed."

Noah's face fell.

6

RISE AND SHINE...

Seven and a Half Days Until the Election

The closet wasn't exactly comfortable. Future reluctantly gave Noah the bed's fluffiest pillow and his backpack for extra head support, but sleep remained a challenge. Noah curled up under the purple blanket his mother made the summer she thought she would enjoy knitting. The raggedy thing barely covered his body, and the floor was hard. But what truly kept him awake were the possibilities racing through his mind. He was going to be popular—and soon! And he'd be president, just like Paul. He couldn't wait to hear what Future had planned. Eventually, after some toss-ing, turning, and envisioning, Noah fell asleep.

He was up and out of the closet before his alarm went off. It was still dark when he shook Future awake.

Future popped up on his elbows and looked around the room, disoriented. "What's wrong?"

Noah smiled and whispered, "I was thinking I should slip into the shower before Mom and Dad wake up. You can go next."

Future shook his head and dropped to his pillow. "Go back to bed, Noah. We can sleep in today."

Noah frowned. "But what about the campaign? Don't I need to get to school early to pass out buttons?"

Future pulled the comforter over himself. "Why? We both know that hasn't been remotely effective." He rolled toward the wall. "Go to sleep. We're getting a late start this morning."

"A late start?" He was never late to anything. "Are you sure?"

Future shut his eyes. "Positive. Get back in the closet."

Noah opened his mouth to protest but closed it. Maybe he should stop worrying for once and follow someone else's lead. And who better to follow than himself? He could cer-tainly use the sleep. Noah shrugged and crept back into the closet, gently closed the door behind himself, and lay down under the tiny blanket.

He fell asleep in seconds.

Noah was shaken awake several hours later. Future, showered and ready, crouched over him holding a steaming white mug with Noah's school picture from first grade printed across the front. Noah wiped the sleep from his eyes. Future passed him the cup.

"What time is it?" Noah asked.

"School started fifteen minutes ago."

Noah's eyes bulged. He leapt to his feet, spilling a few drops of hot liquid on the way up. "Ow!" he yelped, and rubbed where the drink had scalded his leg.

"Take it easy," Future said. "We're getting a late start today, remember? Mom and Dad left about an hour ago. I said we'd—I mean, *I'd*? Or, um, *you'd*? Walk to school. Don't worry. Everything's going according to plan."

Noah caught his breath. "Are you sure?"

"Of course."

Noah nodded his thanks. Took a sip from the mug and cringed. "What is this, tea?"

"Yeah."

"I thought it was gonna be hot chocolate. This is disgusting."

"You have to get used to drinking it. It's another acquired taste."

"Why?"

"Trust me. Finish the tea and hop in the shower. I'm gonna watch TV in the living room."

Noah inspected the mug. Took another sip and cringed again. "I have to finish all of it?"

"All of it," Future said, and headed to the door. "And don't worry about breakfast this morning. I have a plan."

Thirty minutes later, Noah and Future sat in a booth at Baxter's Diner. Classic rock pumped through the speakers in the rafters while bacon and potatoes sizzled on a grill behind the counter. A waitress in an apron dropped off two menus.

"Can we start with one black tea and a hot chocolate, please?" Future asked.

Noah winced.

"You got it," the waitress said, and hurried off to help another table.

"Do I really need to drink more tea?"

Future assessed Noah across the booth. "You do. And I can't stress enough how important it is that you like it."

"Can't I just pretend?"

"We're a terrible actor and you almost dry-heaved when I put in that order."

"*Fine.*" Noah grabbed a menu and perused the specials. "Looks good. I've never been here."

"I know. I found this place yesterday. We're here so no one recognizes us. That's why we're so far from our house and school."

"Oh. Smart."

Future folded his hands on the table while Noah flipped through the menu. "Get the corned beef hash."

"I love corned beef hash."

Future rolled his eyes. "*I know.* Noah, just assume I'm aware of everything you've ever done—or even thought—up until you saw me at the bowling alley."

"Right. Yeah, that makes sense." Noah turned to the mini jukebox on their table and shuffled through the catalog of songs. "By the way, how am I going to slip into class this morning without a note?"

"You're not."

"What do you mean?"

"You're getting trash duty today."

Noah stopped playing with the jukebox and stared down Future. "What? I have to pick up garbage with the trouble-makers after school?"

"All the popular kids have trash duty this afternoon. You'll be there, too."

"Why?"

Future shrugged. "They get in trouble for skipping gym or something."

"No, not why do *they* need to have trash duty. Why do *I*?"

Future sighed. "I told you, you need to be popular to win the election. This is the first step. You're going to go to trash duty and say nothing."

"Nothing? Not even hi?"

"You can say hi. But then you need to pretend to sleep on the bench behind the gym."

"Won't I get into more trouble?" Noah asked.

"Will you just trust me? Coach Hawkins doesn't actually care how much trash anyone picks up. He hands out bags, then goes to his office to watch old football games on TV or something."

"Huh." Noah held a finger to his forehead. "So you want me to get trash duty and pretend to take a nap? How is that going to help me win the election?"

"Because it'll make it seem like getting in trouble is no

big deal to you. And if the popular kids think you don't care, they'll think you're cool."

Noah stared at Future. "That's it?"

"That's it."

"It sounds kind of dumb."

"It's *very* dumb. But this is how the world works."

Noah leaned back in the booth. "You really think I can get the popular kids to like me enough to vote for me?"

"It'll be a lot of work, but yes. And if the popular kids vote for you, all the kids who want to be popular will vote for you, too. And that's how you're going to be class president next year."

Noah dreamed of what lay ahead and a smile crept across his face. But then his smile vanished. "Why won't they vote for Gregg? He's the most popular kid in school."

Future chuckled. "Don't worry about Gregg."

"But he's captain of the basketball team and was the seventh-grade king of the Winter Jubilee."

"Gregg's going to drop out of the election next week."

Noah's mouth fell open. A black tea and a hot chocolate were placed on the table. "You boys know what you want?" the waitress asked.

"We'll have two orders of corned beef hash," Future said.

"How do you want the eggs?" she asked.

"Sunny-side up. And sourdough toast, please," Noah and Future said.

The waitress jotted down the order and raised her eyebrows as she left. "Twins always weird me out."

"Why would Gregg quit?" Noah asked. "Is there some sort of scandal?"

Future shook his head. "He didn't know student government meets after school. He can't be president and go to basketball practice. He chooses basketball."

Noah scrunched up his face. "What do you mean he didn't know government meets after school? Principal Thompson told us twice in our election kickoff meeting. It was basically the only thing we discussed other than the speech and the rules for the debate. It was even on that letter they had our parents sign."

Future shrugged. "I don't know what to tell you. Gregg doesn't listen. He's going to drop out next week. And the popular kids think Claire Trotter is nice, but they're not really friends with her. This election is about to be wide open."

"And today I just have to pretend to sleep during trash duty?"

"Yep. And hold on to this." Future reached into his pocket and passed a blue ballpoint pen across the table.

Noah stared at the pen, perplexed. "What do I need this for?"

"You'll know. Just be ready."

7

THE PLAN BEGINS...

One Week and Three Hours Until the Election

Noah and Future sat next to each other on the bus after breakfast. It was Noah's first time riding public transportation. While Future explained what incredible bargains their recently purchased bus passes were, Noah slouched and stole glances at the passengers hopping on and getting off at each stop. What if someone he knew saw him with Future? What would he even say?

"Don't worry," Future said, "we're not going to see anyone we know on this bus."

Noah eyed Future. Was he reading his mind?

"I'm not reading your mind," Future said. "I know how you think. How many times do I have to remind you we're the same person?"

Noah nodded. "Right…But how do you know we're not going to see anyone?"

"Well, first off, everyone our age is already at school, and most of Mom and Dad's friends are at work. But more importantly, I know because I've already lived this morning and ridden this bus."

Noah furrowed his brow. "*This* bus? Like, now?"

"Yeah. Don't worry about it. Just focus on getting trash duty."

"Ugh." Noah's palms began to sweat. Had he ever been disciplined for anything? He'd never even been late to class without a note. "Do I really have to do this?"

"Trust me," Future said, "it won't be a big deal. And eventually the punishment and the crime will be forgotten."

Noah sighed and the bus came to a stop a couple of blocks from school.

"Get off here," Future said.

Noah nodded and shook Future's hand. "Good luck," Future said. "I'll lay low at the library across town and see you tonight."

Noah grabbed his backpack and nervously disembarked to walk the rest of the way and face his fate. Somehow even hours after the day began there was traffic in the drop-off line. Noah exhaled and climbed the front steps to the school.

He strolled into Ms. Tucker's third-period Pre-Algebra class twenty-three minutes after the bell. His friends seemed shocked to see him arriving late. Darnell gave him an are-you-okay salute, and Samar offered a where-have-you-been shrug. Ms. Tucker glanced up from her desk while the class worked through equations in their textbooks. "Thanks for joining us, Mr. Nicholson. I assume you have a note?"

Noah took a deep breath to prepare for the punishment ahead. "I do not."

Gregg and the kids at the back of the class chuckled.

Ms. Tucker sighed. "Fine. Take a seat. We're doing the problems on page eighty-seven this morning. Let me know if you have any questions."

Noah stepped toward the exit and processed her words. He spun back to Ms. Tucker and blinked. "What?"

"Take a seat." Ms. Tucker turned to a book on her desk.

"You want me to sit down?" Noah asked.

"Please," Ms. Tucker said.

Noah's heart pounded. Future's plan was unraveling

before it had begun. "You don't want me to go to the office to sign up for trash duty after school?"

"I assume you have a good reason for being late. Sit down and try to catch up." Ms. Tucker flipped a page in her book.

Noah checked the ground to make sure his feet were planted firmly. He clenched his thumbs in his fists. "But I don't have a good reason. I'm late because I slept in and went to breakfast."

Samar's and Darnell's eyes went wide. Lucy tilted her head and grinned.

Ms. Tucker frowned. "Typically, that would be information a student kept to themself."

"Well, now you know," Noah said.

Ms. Tucker nodded. "Yep. Now I know."

Noah turned his palms out. "So…?"

"So take a seat," Ms. Tucker said.

"Yeah, Noah," Gregg teased. "Take a seat."

"Some of us are trying to learn here," Perry said with a smile.

Gregg and his friends laughed.

Noah felt sweat forming on his brow. "I…can't."

"Of course you can," Ms. Tucker said.

Noah's heart beat faster. "This isn't how this is supposed to go."

"Luckily this is my class and I run it how I choose. And I choose for you to proceed with my assignment."

Noah stood frozen. What was he supposed to do now?

Ms. Tucker seemed to sense his confusion. "Sit."

Noah's head felt light. "Ms. Tucker, is this really how you'd like to handle my situation?"

Ms. Tucker rubbed her forehead. "Noah, what exactly is your concern this morning?"

"My concern? My concern is..." Noah's eyes drifted. What Future would do? Wait. He *was* Future. Basically. So anything he would do would be what Future did. Possibly.

He glanced at his classmates. Half of them seemed somewhat intrigued by his next move, while the other half had already lost interest and returned to the assignment. And that was all the motivation he required: Noah needed to be noticed. He took a deep breath and turned to his teacher.

"My concern is how this room is being run. I'm worried our math class, which only yesterday was a respected—no, *admired*—beacon of middle school learning, is becoming a lawless land without consequences. And if we don't recognize and punish tardiness for the crime it is, we'll be on a slippery slope to absolute anarchy and our entire educational system and way of life will be in jeopardy. It'll only be a matter of time until no students come to school at all, and we'll all spend our days loitering outside burger joints, occasionally wandering in without shoes or even shirts and expecting service. And Ms. Tucker, that's just not something we can let happen."

Ms. Tucker stared at Noah.

Noah stared back.

He had the class's attention.

"Keep your shirt on. Take a seat," Ms. Tucker said.

Noah felt like he'd gotten the wind knocked out of him. He looked to the empty desk next to Samar and Darnell. His friends frantically gestured to the open chair, wanting to bring an end to the shenanigans. He hung his head and took a step to the desk, but he couldn't bring himself to take another. He glanced over his shoulder and spotted a wastebasket by the door. Before Noah could process what he was doing, he strode to the basket and picked it up.

"Don't do it," Samar said.

Noah gave Samar a toothless smile and raised his shoulders, apologizing in advance. He tipped the wastebasket upside down and dumped its contents to the floor. Thirty mouths dropped open in bewilderment, Samar's and Darnell's widest of all.

Ms. Tucker closed her eyes and bit her lip. "Okay. You have trash duty."

Gregg and Perry nodded, seemingly impressed.

Noah sighed, relieved. "Thank you, Ms. Tucker." He took a knee next to the litter. "Let me pick this up. It'll be good practice for this afternoon. Sorry about the mess."

Noah tossed the rubbish into the bin and glanced up across the room to find Lucy watching him. She shook her head, but she was smiling.

After math, Noah watched Samar and Darnell cautiously approach him in the crowded hall. Did they think he was going to explode? He figured he was more likely to faint. The school had been spinning since he'd gone to the office to sign up for his punishment.

Samar blew air through his teeth. "Well, that was interesting."

Darnell nodded. "Yeah, Noah, is there something you need to tell us? Is everything okay at home? And in life?"

Noah made his way toward the cafeteria. It felt like his body was on autopilot. "Everything is okay."

His friends didn't look reassured. They followed him down the hall.

"What got into you back there?" Samar asked.

"Yeah," Darnell said. "What were you doing?"

Noah shrugged. "Campaigning?"

Samar recoiled. "Campaigning?"

Darnell wrinkled his nose. "We thought you, um, came to your senses and…dropped out of the race?"

"Nope," Noah said.

Samar sighed. "Honestly, I got excited when I didn't see you in front of the school with Gregg and Claire this morning. But it seems you've found a way to make your already disastrous campaign worse. Kudos if that's been your intention all along. Is that it? Has this all been an elaborate joke or some performance piece for Drama?" Samar appeared hopeful.

Noah shook his head. "No, I'm serious about the election. I want to win. But I realized what I'd been doing wasn't working, so I'm trying something new."

Samar frowned. "Dumping trash on Ms. Tucker's floor is definitely new."

"Certainly different, right?" Darnell said. "To me it didn't quite scream 'Vote for Noah for class president,' but maybe some of our classmates were able to read between the lines?"

"It just doesn't seem like you have a plan," Samar said.

Noah stopped walking and took a deep breath. "Guys, I know what I'm doing. I think. Maybe. Look, I have a plan."

"I mean a *viable* plan," Samar said. "Please quit. Not just for us. For you."

Noah squinted. "I think I need to play this out."

"Couldn't you be reasonable instead?" Darnell asked.

"I am being reasonable. I think I might have stumbled into a very specific path to victory."

Samar sighed. "You're absolutely stumbling. And I'd say it's less like you're on a path to victory and more like you're grasping at straws."

"Just give me a few days," Noah said. "You guys trust me, right?"

Darnell and Samar exchanged concerned looks.

"Hey, Nicholson!" Gregg called.

Noah and the boys turned to Gregg and the basketball team coasting down the hall.

"That was hilarious," Gregg continued. "You're a nut."

Gregg's friend Perry gave Noah a friendly slap on the back. "Legendary, Noah. Definitely the highlight of my week."

Noah offered a big smile and nod in return.

Samar and Darnell stared at Gregg and Perry, bewildered, and the basketball team moseyed on.

Noah lifted his chin.

Darnell scratched the back of his head and whispered, "Were Gregg and Perry just nice to you?"

"Yep," Noah said.

Samar and Darnell continued to stare at the taller boys entering the cafeteria.

"You might be on to something," Samar said.

Noah beamed.

8

A GLUTTON FOR PUNISHMENT...

Six Days and Twenty-Two Hours Until the Election

Coach Hawkins taught physical education and oversaw the boys' athletic teams. As far as Noah could tell, Hawkins's blue baseball cap had been surgically attached to his head and his plastic clipboard was superglued to his left hand.

Noah stood on the grassy field behind the gym holding an orange trash bag next to half the basketball team, two popular girls from the dance team who had never spoken to him, the kid who had repeated sixth grade three times, and the boy who never showed up to English class. The field surrounded an asphalt basketball court and was used on Fridays when the PE classes ran the mile, and each afternoon by the eighth graders at lunch. Unfortunately, the eighth graders weren't the best at throwing their lunches away, so Principal Thompson had replaced detention with trash duty.

Coach Hawkins frowned at his clipboard and then frowned harder at the group. "Most of you know the drill. It's not rocket science. Spend the next hour picking up all the litter you come across on this field and we'll call it time served. I don't care if you talk to each other, but I do care if you're not working."

Noah gave a friendly smile to the popular girl with the braids. "Hi, I'm Noah. This is my first time getting into trouble." The girl rolled her eyes at her friend. Noah clenched his teeth.

Coach Hawkins shook his head. "Also, no horseplaying. Just because there's a basketball on the court doesn't mean this should turn into an informal practice. I'm serious, guys. And I'm disappointed you're here again."

Gregg squeezed the back of his neck. "Sorry, Coach."

"It happens," Hawkins said with a shrug. "Okay, I'm going to my office to catch up on paperwork. See you in an hour." Hawkins took another look at his clipboard, frowned again, and headed to the gym.

"I wonder what kind of paperwork he has," Noah

whispered to the English-class-skipper. "What do you think? Order forms for dodgeballs and gym shorts?"

The boy ignored him and wandered into the field, picking up candy wrappers and soda cans. The popular kids giggled about something and scooped trash into their bags.

Noah exhaled and turned to the steel bench behind him. It didn't seem like the most comfortable place to rest. Even worse than his closet. The longer he stared at the bench, the sillier his plan seemed. Or was it Future's plan? He folded his orange trash bag into a makeshift pillow and lay on the bench. He wasn't sure if the "pillow" made the bench more comfortable, but at least it was clean. He closed his eyes and pretended to sleep.

Less than a minute later, he felt a nudge on his shoulder. He opened his eyes to find the girl with the braids and the other popular kids staring down at him.

"Are you taking a nap?" she asked.

Noah's heart raced. He wanted more than anything to play it cool. For once in his life. Not trusting what would come out of his mouth, he only shrugged.

"Awesome," she said. "I'm Zuri."

"Noah," he said, and closed his eyes again.

"Wow," Gregg said with a laugh. "Had no idea Noah was such a rebel."

"Legend," Perry said.

Noah kept his eyes shut and bit the inside of his lip to keep from smiling. He listened to the chuckles and footsteps of the group strolling away. And he listened to the breeze and enjoyed the sun. When was the last time he'd simply relaxed? It felt nice. He felt another nudge.

Noah looked up to find Coach Hawkins glaring down.

"You're kidding me, right?" Hawkins asked.

Noah cringed and sat up. "I thought you said you were going to do paperwork in your office."

"I thought I told you to pick up trash."

Noah nodded. "Call it even?"

"Nice try, kid." Hawkins eyed his clipboard. "I'm writing you up for trash duty again tomorrow."

"*Again?*" Noah hopped to his feet. "But tomorrow is Friday."

"Not how I like kicking off my weekend either." The coach grimaced at a pad of disciplinary slips on his clipboard, patted the pockets on his shorts, and came up empty-handed. "I forgot my pen."

Noah groaned, dug into his pants, and handed Hawkins the ballpoint pen from Future.

Later that night, long after he'd settled into bed, Noah was startled awake by the sound of fingers drumming against glass. He fell to the floor, rubbed his eyes, and shuffled to the window. He lifted it to find Future on the lawn wearing the gray sweatshirt and holding something steaming in a paper to-go cup.

"I got you another tea," Future said.

Noah frowned and looked at the clock on his bedside table. "At one in the morning?"

"It's decaffeinated."

Noah eyed the cup hopefully. "Does it taste better that way?"

"Kind of tastes worse."

Noah sighed, reached down and took the cup, and helped Future inside. He shut the window behind him.

"How'd it go today?" Future asked.

"I've been trying to answer that question myself all night." Noah ran a hand through his hair. "Either great or horribly, I guess?"

"Those are usually the two options." Future spun the shiny globe on the desk. "I love this thing."

"Six months' allowance," Noah said.

"I know," Future said. "I thought for sure we'd use it all the time for school, but we haven't needed it once."

Noah nodded. "Fun to play with, though."

"Yep." Future put a finger on the globe to stop it from spinning and took a seat on the bed.

Noah paced in his plaid pajamas. "I'm not sure what I did wrong, but I almost didn't get in trouble with Ms. Tucker."

"Did you dump her wastebasket on the floor?"

Noah stopped pacing. "How did you know?"

Future shrugged. "I did the same thing."

"I thought you might've. Why didn't you just tell me?"

"I don't want to lead you too much. Anything you do needs to feel natural, right? Just trust our instincts and we'll be fine."

"Feels risky," Noah said. "Wouldn't we be better off if you told me everything?"

"I know what we're doing. The more you know ahead of time the less you'll act like yourself in the moment." Future glanced down at his clothes and admired Noah's pajamas. "Can I borrow some PJs? I didn't pack any."

"I only have one clean set left."

"I don't mind," Future said.

Noah blinked, grabbed a pair of flannel pajamas from his dresser, and tossed them to Future.

"Thanks," Future said. He held up the pajamas and made a circle with his index finger. "You mind?"

"Not at all." Noah turned to face the closet. "I'm a little modest, too."

Future began changing into the flannels. "You should clean this place."

Noah eyed the clothes at his feet and nodded. "Do you think you could do a couple loads of laundry while I'm at school tomorrow?"

"Probably shouldn't risk being here during the day too much in case Mom or Dad comes home. Also, I really enjoyed myself at the library. Caught up on some reading. I don't remember the last time I had time to read for fun. You got trash duty again tomorrow, right?"

Noah frowned at the closet. "Um, yeah."

"Then you did great today." Future finished buttoning his pajamas. "Done."

Noah turned. Something didn't feel right. "How did you know Coach Hawkins was going to need a pen?"

Future shrugged. "Because I got in trouble for pretending to sleep, too."

"Really? Why did you think to do that? And how come you rode that bus we took this morning? I've been thinking about it all day. Mom or Dad always gives us a ride to school. Did you—" Noah stopped talking and raised his eyebrows.

"You figured out the answers to those questions yourself, didn't you?" Future asked.

It felt like the air had been sucked out of the room. "This isn't the first time you've gone back in time."

"Bingo," Future said. "We're smart."

Noah swallowed. "How many times have you done this?"

"Gone back in time? Twice. But I've got it all figured out now."

Noah's legs went wobbly. He took a seat on the bed next to Future. "Couldn't you have at least warned me I was going to have to do trash duty again?"

"Felt like too much for you to swallow and I needed you to commit to the plan. I'm trying to ease you into things."

"Well, could you at least not lie to me? You said I wouldn't get into trouble for sleeping on the bench."

"No, I didn't. I said Coach Hawkins doesn't really care."

Noah shook his head. "Come on, Future. You know that wasn't being totally honest. We need to trust each other." He took a sip of tea and cringed. "This is awful."

"I promise you'll get used to it. And for the record, I do trust you. We need *you* to trust *me*. I'm doing all of this for us. We have a long way to go, and we have to stay on the track I know, or we'll get completely lost. Seriously, the less you know the better. But you're doing great, and we got this. We just have to be cautious of the butterfly effect."

Noah frowned. "What's the butterfly—"

A knock came from the hall. Noah's and Future's faces went white. Future gestured across the room. Noah leapt from the bed and tiptoed to the picture of Four Fingers Finkelstein. A split second later the door swung open, concealing Noah on the other side.

Noah's father stepped into the room wearing a bathrobe. Noah braced himself against the wall and tried to sweat as quietly as possible.

Dr. Nicholson frowned at a frozen Future.

Noah closed his eyes and held his breath.

9

RECONSIDERING BUTTERFLIES...

Six and a Half Days Until the Election

Noah stood like a statue behind his bedroom door. Was his heart thumping loudly enough to wake the neighbors? He could smell his father's aftershave. If they were caught, everything they'd worked toward would be for nothing. He tried to stand firm, but his body quaked.

Dr. Nicholson rubbed his forehead as he stood in the doorway and examined Future sitting on the bed. "Why are you still up, bucko? And are you talking to yourself about butterflies?"

"Oh, um, yeah?" Future forced a laugh. "Presentation for Science class tomorrow about bugs." He lay down and pulled the blanket over himself.

Noah's nose itched and sweat trickled down his brow.

Dr. Nicholson nodded. "Well, it's late. I'm sure you'll do fine. Especially if you get enough sleep. Night." He switched off the light, pulled the door, then paused. "Wait. Bucko?"

Noah tried not to make a sound and concentrated on making himself invisible. Unfortunately, his concentration only made the itch on his nose worse.

"Yeah, Dad?" Future asked.

Noah cringed—he felt a sneeze coming. His nose crinkled and his father opened the door wider. Noah flexed every muscle in his face to avoid sneezing.

"Technically butterflies aren't bugs," Dr. Nicholson said. "They're insects."

"Right," Future said. "Thanks. Love you."

"Goodnight, bucko." Dr. Nicholson closed the door.

Noah stayed propped against his wall, listening to his

father's footsteps saunter down the hall. But he couldn't hold his face still any longer. Noah let out a massive sneeze. He winced and sank to the floor while covering his mouth and nose with both hands.

Future and Noah stared at each other across the room, eyes wide. Noah's heart skipped a beat.

"Bless you," Dr. Nicholson called from the hall.

Future's and Noah's jaws dropped. Future shrugged at Noah and Noah nodded in return.

"Thanks," Future responded. "Night."

The boys listened to their parents' door close. They sat in silence for a few minutes until Noah whispered, "That was close."

"I'll say," Future whispered back.

"We should probably get to sleep," Noah said. "Do you want to hop in the closet?"

The question hung.

"Future?" Noah whispered. "Can you get in the closet?"

"Feels risky. I'm already tucked in and you're right there. I wouldn't want to bang into anything or stumble over the guitar walking across this messy floor."

Noah frowned at the murky room. Any arguing would wake their parents. *"Fine."* He felt his way into the closet, carefully drew the door shut, pulled the tiny blanket over himself, and begrudgingly went to sleep.

Noah was shaken awake at 5:30 AM. He found Future showered and wearing his jacket.

"I'm going to head out," Future whispered. "Meet me in the Mini-Mart parking lot in an hour?"

Noah nodded.

Future pulled a hot mug from behind his back and handed it to Noah.

Noah sighed and took a sip of the tea. He blinked at the cup a few times and a smile crept across his face. "You know, this isn't bad."

"Told you." Future gave Noah a pat on the shoulder and slipped out the window.

After persuading his parents a morning walk would help clear his head, Noah went to the parking lot behind the Mini-Mart.

The lot was busy with commuters pulling in and out to grab coffee and doughnuts, but Future wasn't anywhere to be found. Noah checked inside the store, but he wasn't there either. On his way outside, Noah surprised himself by stopping to buy a black tea. Then he sat on the curb, drank, and waited.

"Psst."

Noah followed the sound to a cinder-block enclosure with a steel gate. He unlatched the gate to find the Mini-Mart's dumpster. It was coated in orange paint that looked like it had been chipping away for decades. Future stood behind the dumpster eating a blueberry muffin.

"It's me," Future said.

Noah stepped inside the enclosure, pulled the gate shut behind him, and smiled. "I can see that." It was comforting to see Future. Like stealing a glance in a mirror and confirming there wasn't anything stuck in his teeth.

Future's eyes lit up. "You got a tea."

Noah took a sip and nodded at the cup. "Just kind of had a craving for one. It really is an acquired taste, I guess."

"One less thing to worry about," Future said.

Noah made a face. "It smells awful in here."

Future stood on his toes and peered into the dumpster. "I think there's expired milk in the bin."

Noah nodded. "That would explain it. So, what's the butterfly effect?"

Future shoved the last third of his muffin in his mouth. "Well," he said with his mouth full. "First off, I'm not entirely sure it's a real problem, but it's this theory Mom and Dad told me about the night they invented time travel." Future pointed at Noah's cup. "Can I get a sip of that?"

Noah handed him the tea. Future took a sip and gave

it back. "Anyway, it's the idea that a butterfly flapping her wings in Oklahoma could cause a tornado three states away."

"Is that how weather works?" Noah asked.

Future squinted. "Maybe? But that's not really the point they were making. The point is, tiny decisions can create chain reactions with huge consequences. Like, if I didn't travel back in time to help you win the election, you wouldn't be drinking tea next to this dumpster. Does that make sense?"

"I think so." Noah tapped a finger against his lips. "So, like, if I fail Ms. Tucker's next math test, I'll never get into Harvard like Paul?"

"Exactly," Future said. "Wow, you really get it."

Noah smirked, like he'd impressed someone he wanted to be friends with. "Thanks. I guess we're the only ones who do get it, right?"

"Totally," Future said with a nod. "And because I've already gone through this stuff a few times, I can guide you away from any potential problems. If something happens that sends us in the wrong direction, I'll just tell you how to course-correct. So, my gut is that as far as the butterfly effect goes, there's probably nothing to worry about."

"Really?"

"Absolutely," Future said.

Someone hoisted a metal trash can over the other side

of the cinder-block wall with a clang and shook its contents into the dumpster. The trash can was pulled back over the wall, and a banana peel and a purple candy wrapper fell out onto Noah's head.

Noah closed his eyes and took a deep breath.

Future cringed. "Listen, I don't think we need to take that as some kind of sign. This is the first time we've spoken next to this dumpster, so I didn't know that was going to happen." He picked up the Coconut Chaos wrapper and smiled. "Hey, look, Samar and Darnell were wrong. We're not the only ones who eat these."

Noah pulled the banana peel off his head and chucked it into the dumpster. "Great…"

Future scratched the back of his neck. "Actually, this might be the wrapper to the one I ate in front of the store the other day."

Noah clenched his jaw. "So, what do I need to do today other than pick up trash after school?"

"There's a pop quiz in Ms. Tucker's class."

"A pop quiz?" Noah massaged his temples. "Are you kidding? Why didn't you tell me to study last night? I'm in trouble in math, remember?"

Future grinned. "You don't have to study. There's going to be a bonus problem at the bottom of the quiz, and anyone who answers it correctly gets an A."

Noah lifted a hand in the air and gave Future a high five. "Fantastic! So what's the question?"

"Something about acorns."

Noah's face dropped. "I'm not a squirrel. I'm going to need more than that."

"Hold your horses, I'm getting to it." Future brushed muffin crumbs off his hands into the dumpster. "The question goes something like, 'If there are so-and-so many acorns and you take away five, how many do you have?'"

Noah blinked at Future. "That's it? Well, how many do you start with?"

"It doesn't matter."

"Right. Because I just subtract five."

Future sighed. "No. Five is the answer."

"You said you take away five," Noah said, and frowned.

"Right. If you *take* five, you have five. It's a trick question."

Noah slowly smiled. "That's kind of smart."

"Yep."

Noah's smile faded. "Did I get that right when I—um, *you* took the test the first time?"

"That's not important," Future said. "The important thing is that you stop by the tea shop on Becker Street after trash duty this afternoon. The café with the giant blue tea-kettle sticking out of its roof?"

"I thought that place sold old movie props."

Future scoffed. "You've got a lot to learn."

"You didn't know what it was last week either, Future."

"Fair point." Future crossed his arms. "Anyway, just be there around four thirty. Get a table for two and order a pot of Darjeeling black tea. It's Lucy's favorite."

Noah's skin tingled.

10

TEA FOR TWO...

Six Days Until the Election

To the untrained eye, Noah's Friday was relatively uneventful.

He didn't have a clue how to solve half of the problems on his math quiz, but he nailed the bonus question. Ms. Tucker seemed relieved when she saw his final answer. Though not as relieved as Noah. He kept to himself during trash duty, other than to exchange a smile and a nod with Perry who was also in trouble again.

The most challenging part of his day was convincing

Darnell and Samar that the strain of seventh grade wasn't getting to him. His friends worried his being disciplined two days in a row was the result of spiraling out from pressure. They couldn't wrap their heads around how or why Noah saw it as a campaign strategy, but Noah was loving the results. Little things, like a finger-point from Gregg or a wave in the hall from the kid who never showed up to English, felt monumental to him. And Zuri's invite during lunch to help her and her friends cut shamrocks out of green construction paper for the Spring Fling seemed world-shattering. Even something as tiny as a classmate making eye contact felt like a massive improvement. It might have all been in his head—perhaps these types of things had always happened, and he'd overlooked them— but now Noah Nicholson felt like he belonged. Confident. Accepted. And appreciated. Maybe he really did have a chance to win the school election.

But there were more pressing things to be concerned with: What would he talk about with Lucy that evening? Why couldn't Future have prepared him more? Suggested a few topics of conversation, or even a list of areas to avoid? But the last couple of days had gone more right than wrong. Maybe he should stop worrying, trust Future, and follow his own instincts?

Noah arrived at the tea shop at a quarter after four. The dining room had an enormous clock on the wall with *it's tea time* painted across its face, and a dozen circular wooden tables. He sat himself at a small table in the back, ordered, and waited. Every few minutes the bells on the front door chimed when people came or left, and each time he heard the bells he glanced up expectantly. By the time Lucy arrived, it was five o'clock and Noah had drunk an entire pot of tea.

She stood in the doorway with a raised eyebrow, seemingly amused to see Noah across the room. Her dark hair was in a ponytail. Noah waved. She approached.

"What are you doing here?" Lucy asked.

Noah glanced at his empty cup and shrugged. "I always drink a ton of tea before my Friday-night skydiving lessons."

She smiled. "Oh yeah? You're learning to skydive?"

"I teach, actually. It's through the nursing home. Kind of my way to give back?"

"My grandmother would love that kind of thing. Would it be okay if she quilted her own parachute?"

"I would encourage it."

Lucy tapped her fingernails on the chair across from Noah. "We keep running into each other, don't we?"

"It's almost like the universe is trying to get us together."

93

Noah's eyes went wide. Why had he been so forward? Should he say he was joking? "I, um, mean—"

"Mind if I wait with you until my friend gets here?" Lucy pulled out the chair and sat.

Noah swallowed and gestured to a server for another round of tea and an extra teacup.

"What are you having?" Lucy asked.

"Darjeeling tea," he said.

Her eyes went wide. "Really? That's my favorite."

"Oh? Mine, too." Noah felt his hands shaking so he slid them onto his knees. It was mostly nerves, but the caffeine didn't help.

Lucy eyed Noah. "You're not like I thought."

"Yeah?"

"Yeah."

Noah swallowed. "What am I like?"

She crinkled her nose. "I'm not sure yet. But I thought I had you figured out. I've known you since the third grade."

"Second," Noah corrected. He flinched. Had he spoken too quickly?

The server delivered a fresh pot of hot water, another cup, and two tea bags. Noah offered his thanks and poured for Lucy and himself.

"So what was yesterday all about?" Lucy asked.

He placed the pot back on the table. "Trying something new I guess."

"Did you drop out of the election? I haven't seen you in front of the school the last couple of days."

Noah blushed and tried not to smile while he imagined Lucy looking for him in the morning. It wasn't until he noticed her staring at him expectantly that he remembered she'd asked a question. "Oh! I'm still running. Just trying something new there, too."

Lucy smiled, and Noah eyed the cloud of tea expanding in his cup.

"I don't know anyone else our age who likes tea," she said. "My friend Maria always gets hot chocolate when we come here."

Noah shrugged. "Tea can be an acquired taste for some people."

"I suppose," she said. "How did you acquire it?"

"Me?" Noah rested a hand on his bouncing knee. "I guess...I think maybe I've always loved it?"

"You love it?" She frowned. "I mean, I like tea, but I wouldn't say I love it."

Noah sank in his chair.

She pulled the tea bag out of her cup with a spoon. "I drink tea on Fridays after choir practice so I can stay awake long enough to say goodnight to my mom when she gets home. She and her brother—my uncle—own a restaurant together. It's called Nopal? They serve contemporary Mexican food. She's the manager and he's the chef. There was an article in the paper about them a few weeks ago. Did you see it? My uncle dyed his hair green for the photoshoot. I'm not sure I've ever seen him with his natural hair color except in pictures of him with my mom when they were younger."

"I didn't see it," Noah said. "But that's cool."

"I probably wouldn't have seen the article either if my mom didn't tell me. She always says not enough people read the paper anymore, so we flip through it together during breakfast before she takes me to school."

"Maybe I should do that, too."

"You should," she said. "You never know what you could accidentally stumble across. That's another thing my mom says."

Noah smiled and she smiled back. The bells on the door rang and Lucy turned to see her friend Maria step into the café. Maria appeared confused to see Lucy with Noah.

Noah gave a friendly wave but felt his heart sink. He was about to be abandoned.

Lucy dug into her pocket and placed a few dollars in front of him. "For the tea."

Noah pushed the money back across the table when she stood. "Take it. This is on me."

She shook her head. "No way. I crashed your table. Thanks for keeping me company. Good luck with your sky-diving class."

And with a wink, Lucy crossed the room to join her friend.

He watched her go with a sigh and drifted to the counter to pay the check. On his way out the door, he tried to wave goodbye, but Lucy was deep in conversation with Maria. They were laughing about something, but he couldn't tell what. Hopefully it wasn't about him.

With a jingle of the bells, Noah made his way out and headed home. During the walk, he replayed his interaction with Lucy in his head again and again. Was there anything he could have said to make their conversation last a little longer? Why couldn't life have a do-over button? But then again, life *did* have a do-over button. And it was becoming clear how lucky he was to have Future pressing it. After all, he was the only one who knew how much Noah liked Lucy. He'd even gone through the trouble of training him to enjoy tea and setting up the date. Future was turning out to be a real friend. The thought brought a smile to Noah's face.

When he turned onto his street it finally occurred to him his drink with Lucy might have gone okay. Or, dare he say, even good? Maybe Lucy didn't have a date to the

Spring Fling dance. Maybe he should ask her. Maybe she'd say yes.

Suddenly, a hand reached across the sidewalk and yanked him through a wall of hedges.

"Didn't mean to startle you," Future said from behind the shrubbery. "We've got a huge problem."

11

BIG TROUBLE...

Five and a Half Days Until the Election

Noah brushed twigs and leaves off his shirt and oriented himself. He and Future stood on their neighbors' lawn. He'd never gotten a good look at their blue stucco house—it had been enclosed by shrubs that stretched over his head as long as he could remember. It could use a fresh coat of paint. A few of the shutters framing its windows appeared ready to fall off. Two rusty lounge chairs sat in the middle of the overgrown lawn and an oil spot took up most of the driveway. But the hedges were perfectly maintained. Well, they had been until Future pulled him through a hole that wasn't intended to be child-size. Noah eyed Future and whispered, "Why were you hiding in the bushes?"

"We don't have to whisper," Future said. He pointed a thumb at the blue house. "Mr. and Mrs. Crusham went to Cincinnati to see their grandkids this afternoon."

"How do you know?"

"I helped them pack their car."

Noah frowned. "Isn't that a little dangerous?"

"They thought I was you," Future said with a shrug. "And I knew you wouldn't be home until around now."

Noah sighed. "Still seems reckless."

"It's not like I snuck into our house at dinnertime to play the guitar in the living room. Do you have any idea how lonely I am? We're not allowed to talk in the library, and it's not like you and I get to spend much time together. Have some compassion. I'm doing this for us, remember? And we've got a bigger problem than me helping our elderly neighbors."

"Okay. Sorry. What's wrong?"

Future took a deep breath. "Mom and Dad aren't going to invent time travel."

Noah blinked. "*What*? Why? How do you know?"

"Because you didn't break the blender this afternoon."

Noah squinted at Future. "So?"

"So?" Future crossed his arms. "I told you getting a new blender was the thing that gave Mom her epiphany—her big realization how traveling through time could be possible? But now she won't have her epiphany, so she and Dad won't invent their time machine."

"Because I didn't break the blender?"

"Right," Future said. "You were supposed to make a milkshake after school. But this afternoon you had tea with Lucy after trash duty instead."

Noah threw his hands in the air. "Because you told me to have tea with Lucy!"

"Fair. Yeah, I probably should've reminded you. I completely forgot. Ugh. How'd tea go, by the way?"

Noah turned up his palms modestly. "Maybe not bad?"

"Really?"

"Yeah. I was thinking I might ask her to the dance."

"You should," Future said quickly.

"Seriously?"

"That's part of the reason I wanted you to have tea with her. I think it would be fun to go to a dance. And it'd be nice for me to have a date lined up when I got home. Wow, I still can't believe you had tea with Lucy."

Noah frowned. "Didn't you have tea with her last week?"

Future made a circle in the Crushams' overgrown lawn

with his shoe. "No. I overheard next week that she had tea today and Maria ran late."

Noah squinted at Future. "How much of this stuff that you've been having me do have you tried?"

"Most of it. If I did all of it, I'd be class president already and I wouldn't have needed to travel back in time to guide you. But because I've done this a couple times already, I know what works and what doesn't. You just have to trust me. I've worked hard to get us where we are and to know where we need to go."

Noah considered everything that Future had helped with already—they'd avoided a potentially disastrous pop quiz in math, Gregg and his crew were becoming friendly, and his relationship with Lucy was improving by the day.

And Future was the only person who really knew how much that stuff mattered to him, which made sense because he *was* him.

Noah scratched the back of his neck. "Yeah, you're right. Um. Thank you."

"No problem," Future said. "But none of it matters if we can't get Mom and Dad back on the path to make a time machine."

Noah nodded. They were in this together. "Okay. Understood. Let's problem solve. What did you do this afternoon? Originally."

"I got hungry after school and made a milkshake. And I left the blender on the edge of the counter."

"Dad hates that," Noah said.

"I know. When Dad came in from the study, he shut the door a little too hard and the blender smashed on the ground. We scrubbed up the mess, then went to the mall to buy a new one."

"And Mom has her big realization tonight?" Noah asked.

"Tomorrow," Future said. "After she and Dad make smoothies. That's when she'll notice the new blender's reverse button. But now that our blender didn't break, she's not going to have her epiphany."

"The butterfly effect," Noah muttered.

"Bingo."

Noah began pacing around the lawn. "Can't I just make a milkshake now?"

"Nuh-uh," Future said. "Mom and Dad are home and Dad's already making dinner."

"Shoot." Noah lowered his head and grimaced. "I can't wait for Gourmet May to be over."

"We've got bigger fish to fry," Future said. "By the way, Dad tries frying a fish tomorrow night. Only eat the mashed potatoes and corn."

Noah nodded. "Thanks for the tip."

"Welcome."

"Can I make a milkshake after dinner?" Noah asked.

"Not tonight. Mom picked up a pie on her way home from work."

"At least she didn't try baking one."

Future sighed. "That reminds me, she bakes cookies on Sunday and brings them out as a surprise. Dad's chicken is going to be awful that night, but it's better than the cookies. Eat as much of the chicken as you can and make a big deal about how full you are."

"Got it." Noah stopped pacing. "Wait. If Mom and Dad aren't going to create time travel, wouldn't you disappear or something?"

Future shook his head. "I think it's worse than that."

"Worse how?" Noah asked.

"I was flipping through a book in the library, and I came across a theory that proposes that if I'm still here by the time I originally left to travel back in time, all the matter in my body will explode, creating a domino effect infinitely more powerful than an atomic bomb. It could mean the end of the universe."

Noah went pale. "Wow."

"Yeah." Future sat in one of the rusty lounge chairs and stared at the hedges. "It was a novel about an intergalactic war between humans and worm-people, but still."

Noah stared at Future. "Okay, so that outcome feels unlikely, then."

"Well, if I'm stuck here, we'll have to take turns sleeping in the closet for the rest of our lives. The universe might as well explode."

Noah exhaled. "This is an important blender."

"*Very* important," Future said. "You better figure out how to break the one you have."

12

A DISASTROUS DISAPPOINTMENT...

Five Days Until the Election

Noah tried to sleep in the next morning, but the growling from his stomach and anxiety from the lack of an impending time machine made it impossible. Future had been right about the raspberry pie their mother brought home—it was delicious, but he couldn't eat more than a few bites of the rest of dinner and went to bed hungry.

After failing to ignore the grumbles from his belly,

Noah sat up and peered around his empty room. Future had planned to stay out of sight by heading to the library bright and early to wait for it to open. That meant it was up to Noah to trigger his mother's epiphany. So, at 6:15 AM he rolled out of bed to make a milkshake and break the blender.

Noah rounded the corner to the kitchen and jumped. His father sat at the counter, grading tests.

"You're up early," Dr. Nicholson said.

Noah squeezed his eyes shut. Busted. "I was gonna have a milkshake."

Dr. Nicholson tossed his pen onto his pile of exams and walked to the fridge. "Don't be ridiculous. That's an awful way to start the day. Let me cook you some eggs."

Noah bit his lip. He was famished, but unfortunately there was no version of his father using the blender to make eggs. He took a seat and watched his father cook.

"How's math?" his father asked.

"I aced our pop quiz yesterday." It felt good to say at first, but then not so good when he recalled he'd only gotten the A because Future gave him the answer to the bonus question.

"That's outstanding!" his father said. "Looks like the work you're putting into studying instead of campaigning is paying off."

"I'm campaigning, too."

"Are you?" Dr. Nicholson sounded disappointed.

"I am. And things are picking up in the polls."

Dr. Nicholson's forehead wrinkled. "I'm surprised your middle school does polling."

"It's unofficial."

"Ah," his father said. "Well, good. Elections are tricky. Even with professional politics you never really know what'll happen."

Noah raised his chin and pulled his shoulders back, imagining himself as confident as Paul. "I'm going to be class president."

Dr. Nicholson nodded. "Your mother and I will love you no matter what happens."

Noah dropped his shoulders. "That's something you'd say if you weren't sure I'd win."

His father sighed and seemed to take a moment to choose his words carefully. "I'm sure you have a real shot, but school elections are tough."

"Paul won."

Dr. Nicholson nodded at the frying pan. "Yep. He did. And he worked really, really hard. Just like you. And maybe he got a little lucky. Who's to say? And who knows what'll happen with your election? No one can see the future, bucko."

Noah smiled. That last part was only partially true.

Dr. Nicholson turned off the burner and shook the eggs

off the pan and onto a plate. "Anyway, what I'm trying to say is we're impressed by everything you're doing. You're juggling a lot of *eggs*—figuratively speaking. Just know it's okay if some of them drop and break along the way. Especially if you're deciding which ones."

Noah grabbed a fork and dug into his breakfast. "Thanks, Dad."

His father nodded, moved the pan to the sink, and grabbed the dish soap.

Noah's eyes went wide. An idea struck. "Why don't you leave that? I can wash it."

"You? Clean?"

"It's the least I can do since you made me breakfast."

His father eyed him. "Who are you and what have you done with my son?"

Noah laughed. "Come on...I clean!"

"Maybe you'll clean your room this afternoon?"

Noah shrugged. "We'll see."

Dr. Nicholson smiled. He left the pan in the sink, took a seat next to Noah, and resumed his grading. When Noah finished eating, he scrubbed his plate and the frying pan. He dried the pan, opened the cabinet above the sink, and peeked at his father who was busy analyzing a test. Noah eyed the blender on the shelf. He took a quick breath and slammed the frying pan into the blender. *Clang!*

The blender didn't break. Noah frowned.

His father barely glanced up from the counter. "Careful, bucko."

"Sorry," Noah said. "Clumsy…"

Noah sighed, placed the pan on the shelf, and slunk away to watch television in the living room.

At lunch Noah suggested his parents make smoothies—like Future said they did during *his* Saturday. It'd be the perfect opportunity for another "accident." But his parents weren't in the mood for smoothies. Noah blinked. Was that a butterfly fluttering by the living room window?

After lunch, Noah's parents slipped away to work so he made a shake. He finished and sat the blender on the edge of the counter, then waited for his father to leave the study and shut the door. But his mother stepped out first. She spied the messy counter and insisted Noah clean up right away.

"And Noah, do your laundry. Your bedroom is a mess, and pretty soon you won't have any clean clothes to wear."

"I will," he said. "I just have a few things to take care of first."

"Today, please," she said.

Noah nodded, but not sleeping in a closet every other night for the rest of his life was a bigger priority. His mother headed down the hall and he stuck the blender under the running faucet. When the last of the ice cream had trickled down the drain, he took a deep breath, turned off the water, and smashed the blender on the kitchen floor.

"I'm okay!" he called. "Let me get a broom."

Noah couldn't stop smiling while he swept the glass. And he couldn't wait to share the good news. He told his parents he needed to study and made the long walk across town to the main branch of the public library. The automatic doors on the gorgeous white building opened and Noah strolled inside. Sunshine spilled in from the skylights. Why did this place always have such a calming effect on him? Maybe because it was kept so clean? It still felt new even though it was older than he was. It had been years since he'd visited. If only he had the time.

Noah made his way through the children's section and passed rows and rows of fiction. He found Future leaning against the railing of the sunken koi pond in the middle of the library.

Future looked up, pleased to see Noah. "At least once a day one of the little kids at story time makes a break from the magic carpet and tries to climb this railing to swim with the fish."

Noah peered into the pond. Dozens of koi fish floated in a cluster, scales to scales, like they were cuddling for warmth.

"A kid made it in this morning," Future continued. "He couldn't have been older than four, but he outran his dad and two librarians. The other kids in the story circle were cheering and jumping up and down. It got *loud* in here. The kid practically hurdled the fence. He screamed when he hit the pond—probably colder than he expected. Water went everywhere. Luckily, he didn't hurt himself. The librarians just kind of rolled their eyes and got a couple beach towels from the back to dry off the kid and soak up the splash."

"Whoa." Noah eyed the dry floor. "Good thing they had towels."

"Always important to be prepared for anything." Future nodded at the fish. "I ran over from the reference room as soon as it happened, but they all seemed fine. Could you imagine a baby elephant crashing into our living room? Must've been like that, right? But none of the fish panicked. They just kept floating. I figure they felt safe because they had each other."

Noah smiled. "I was thinking the same thing." He looked around the library and squinted at Future leaning against the railing. "You look right at home here. Like a regular."

Future smiled and shrugged.

"It's weird," Noah continued. "I mean, you've been hanging out in this place that I've always liked but never make the time to visit. And it feels like—I don't know, like maybe in another life it could be my place, too? And now here we are together." Noah shook his head. "That sounded dumb. I'm rambling. Maybe I don't know what I mean."

"No. I get it." Future patted Noah on the back. "We speak the same language."

Noah smiled. He looked at Future, cocked his head, and bit his lip. "Been a weird year with Paul gone, hasn't it? Is that okay to say out loud?"

Future nodded. "I knew I was going to miss him, but I didn't realize how different the house was going to be."

Noah leaned on the railing and let those words sink in. It was like Future knew his innermost thoughts. Maybe it was safe to say more? "Yeah, it's like, we've always been in Paul's shadow, but we used to be able to...*hide* in his shadow? Just kind of pipe up at dinner every now and then with a joke, make everyone laugh, then slip out of Paul's limelight?"

"Life used to be easier," Future said.

"Much easier." Noah sighed, relieved that Future got it. "All of a sudden Mom and Dad are constantly focused on us. Prying and judging. *How's school? How's the campaign? How are you doing in Pre-Algebra?* They're always looking over our shoulder to make sure we're doing things right, instead of giving us the space they used to give Paul. It's like they respect him more or something? Obviously I want them to be proud of me, but sometimes I need to handle things myself, and how can I do that without space? We used to barely keep up with Darnell and Samar, but it's so much harder now that we're under the microscope. I mean, I still don't understand why we started using numbers *and* letters in math."

"It's ridiculous," Future said. "Pick a lane."

"Mom even asked how the tournament went the other day," Noah said. "They never cared about bowling when Paul was around."

"I can't believe we rolled a gutter ball," Future mumbled.

"We can still be league champions," Noah said.

"We absolutely can," Future said. "Lots to accomplish next week."

"Lots," Noah repeated, and stared at the cuddling koi. His leg trembled as the pressure steamed inside him. But then he remembered that he wouldn't have to navigate those problems alone as long as Future was around, and the shuddering stopped. "It's good that we can talk about this stuff."

Future nodded. "Really good."

"Oh, I almost forgot what I came to tell you! I broke the blender."

Future smiled. "I knew you would."

Noah's mother went to the appliance store on Sunday and returned with a white box, which she confidently placed on the kitchen counter next to Noah's father, who continued to grade exams. Noah released a happy sigh. Had anyone ever been more relieved to see something enclosed in cardboard? Future would be able to go home! And he'd win the election as icing on the cake.

"The salesman said it was the best one on the market," his mother boasted. "It almost has more horsepower than my first car."

Noah smiled and watched his mother open the box and remove a shiny chrome-and-glass blender with a dozen buttons and two dials.

"Gorgeous, dear," Noah's father said without looking up.

Noah leaned in to inspect the dials and buttons. The huge smile on his face turned into a frown. "It doesn't have a reverse button."

"What?" his mother asked.

Noah's heart pounded. He grabbed the blender and held it in front of his face, rereading the labels on the buttons. "There's no reverse function on this blender. It's supposed to have a reverse."

Dr. and Dr. Nicholson stared at their son. They seemed confused.

"A reverse function?" his father asked.

"Yeah," Noah said. "There needs to be a reverse button."

His parents chuckled and his mother put a hand on his shoulder. "Noah, how would being able to mix backwards create a better blending experience? That would be nonsensical."

"But...we need it."

"Sweetie, I've been teaching graduate-level physics *and* engineering courses since before you were born, so I'm uniquely qualified to respond to this. A reverse function would be a ludicrous feature."

Noah scowled at the blender. "Can we take it back and exchange it?"

"Exchange it? Honey, no. It was on sale, so we can't return it. But it really is supposed to be the best blender on the market. It was the store owner's birthday or something. We got an incredible deal."

Noah felt the room spin. "This is *wrong*."

"Wrong?" his father asked.

"Wrong," Noah said.

"I'm not really sure what you mean," his mother said.

"I mean..." Noah placed the blender on the counter and a hand against the wall to prop himself up. Why hadn't he volunteered to go with his mother to the store? He couldn't believe he had left such a critical element to chance. Hadn't Future said he went to the store with his father the first time around? Was Noah letting the universe unravel? He stared at the blender with regret. "I mean, this isn't the blender we're supposed to have."

"Well, you broke the old one, bucko," his father said. "And that blender didn't have a reverse button either."

"Yeah, but..." Noah shook his head.

His parents exchanged worried glances.

"Why is this important to you, Noah?" his mother asked.

"I thought it might...inspire you?" Noah said.

"You thought I'd be inspired by a blender?" his mother asked.

"Yes?"

"Inspire me to what, honey? Are you feeling okay?"

"I don't know." Noah looked hopefully at the blender. "Does it give you any big, world-altering ideas? For a new invention? Maybe about time?"

Noah's parents frowned at the blender and at their son.

"Honey, I think you should go lie down. You seem more overwhelmed than usual this afternoon."

Noah opened his mouth to protest but couldn't think of anything to say.

13

BIRDS OF
A FEATHER...

Three and a Half Days Until the Election

After lying in bed to clear his head, Noah spent Sunday evening working words and phrases loosely associated with time travel into as many conversations with his mother as he could. He even ducked away to the family's old yellow-paged thesaurus in the study a few times to find different ways to say *reverse*. Sadly, *back*, *retreat*, *U-turn*, *unwind*, *unravel*, and *undo* caused as little inspiration as the new blender.

Future tapped on his window after bedtime to be pulled in, but Noah slipped out instead. The boys strode down the sidewalk and Noah brought Future up to speed. A crescent moon lit the sky and the neighborhood smelled of their father's burnt chicken.

Future shoved his hands into his pockets. "Well, I guess the only thing we can do is keep trying."

Noah sighed. "That's what I figured."

"You've got a big day tomorrow. The election kind of depends on it."

"You mean prepping for the debate on Wednesday?" Noah placed a hand on the back of his neck. "I've been so focused on the blender situation that I haven't even thought about how to get ready."

"Don't worry about the debate. It gets canceled after Gregg drops out and Claire has an allergic reaction."

Noah's eyes went wide. "Claire has an allergic reaction? Is she going to be okay?"

Future waved off Noah's concern. "She'll be fine. Apparently she's allergic to lilies. Someone sends flowers to her homeroom teacher. Claire goes home with the sniffles and a scratchy throat on Wednesday and comes back on Thursday."

"That's good. So, what do I have to do tomorrow?"

"Every time Mr. Jones turns his back to the class in Science you need to quack like a duck."

Noah stopped walking. "Are you kidding? I'm getting trash duty again?"

Future grabbed Noah's shoulder and gave it a gentle tug to get him walking again. "You won't get in trouble. I promise. This is an easy one. You just have to quack."

"But why? It's so stupid."

Future looked offended. "It's silly, not stupid. And everyone loves it. Come on, quacking like a duck is the least you can do after the trouble you caused us this weekend."

"Fine." Noah exhaled. "I really won't get trash duty?"

"You won't."

Noah nodded, accepting his mission. "Anything else?"

Future thought for a moment. "Actually, yeah. After math, Perry yells, 'Hey, it's the flight of the bumblebee' when Katie Frankel runs through the hall—"

"Because she's short?" Noah asked.

"And she's wearing yellow overalls with a black turtleneck. Everyone thinks it's hilarious. You should say it instead."

"Really?"

"Yeah," Future said. "People were still talking about how funny it was days later. Make the joke yours. Just say it before Perry."

"Okay. I guess I can do that." Noah admired the moon while the boys approached their house. "Have any plans for tomorrow?"

"Not really. Just desperately brainstorming ways to influence Mom and Dad to invent time travel so I don't have to live in hiding for the rest of my life."

"Fun."

"Yep."

Noah arrived at school early on Monday morning. He marched past the bottlenecked drop-off line and exchanged cordial nods with Claire in front of her muffin-covered campaign table on his way to the boys' restroom which, as he expected, was empty.

Noah stared at himself in the cracked mirror. His white button-up shirt was freshly ironed. He hadn't worn it since the previous Easter. The sleeves had become borderline too short after a year of growing, but he was running low on clean clothes.

He cleared his throat and released a healthy "quack." It sounded impressive with the restroom's acoustics. Noah was as ready as he was going to be. He walked to Mr. Jones's classroom, took a seat, and waited while the rest of the class slowly filed in.

Mr. Jones had the only room in school that still had a

chalkboard. And because of Mr. Jones's habit of leaning against that board, his sweaters were always covered in chalk dust and smudges. His classroom was decorated with Bunsen burners—which the school hadn't allowed students to use in decades—and a massive periodic table, which wasn't part of the curriculum.

Science was one of the few classes Noah had without Darnell or Samar. They had planned to take it together, but due to a misunderstanding, his friends registered for *Miss* Jones's seventh-grade Science class instead. Being without his friends was a lonely way for Noah to start each day. The class did, however, have the entire basketball team.

As soon as the bell rang, Mr. Jones (who had a toupee that wasn't fooling anyone) launched into a lecture about the electrifying, microscopic world of amoebas and other one-celled organisms. When he turned to grab a piece of chalk, Noah took a deep breath, closed his eyes, and released a tiny "quack."

Someone chuckled from the far side of the room, but most of Noah's classmates shot him odd looks. Noah's cheeks warmed. Mr. Jones didn't react. He simply continued diagramming a cell dividing into two on the chalkboard.

Perhaps Mr. Jones hadn't heard? Noah's pulse raced while his eyes darted left and right. His classmates turned back to the front of the room, already uninterested. He rubbed his face in frustration. Making a duck sound wasn't a high point of his political or academic career. Why would Future think it could make him popular or encourage anyone to vote for him? Maybe he should skip this idea and pay attention to Jones? But Future had sacrificed and risked so much to give him this opportunity…and Noah trusted him. It was worth one more shot.

Noah cleared his throat and released another "quack."

More chuckles this time and more confused looks, too. Mr. Jones paused at the board. Noah held his breath. But Mr. Jones resumed his sketch.

Noah glanced around the room. His classmates stared at him expectantly. Eagerly. Like this was the most exciting thing to happen in the history of science. Gregg and Perry were having trouble containing their smiles. Noah's shoulders drifted back, and he grew more confident. He refocused his attention on Jones's back.

"Quack!" Noah belted.

Noah's classmates bit their lips and covered their eyes, ears, or mouths.

Mr. Jones cleared his throat but kept on drawing.

The other kids eyed Noah, anxiously awaiting what he'd do next. Noah Nicholson had become the most interesting person in East Hills Middle School.

Noah rolled his head on his neck and stared boldly ahead. "QUACK!"

Mr. Jones spun on his heel. His toupee didn't move as quickly and sat more crooked than usual. "Who did that?" he demanded.

Noah and his classmates sank in their seats and became fascinated with their desks.

Mr. Jones tapped his chalk-covered fingers against his temple. "Answer me." He lowered his hand to reveal a forehead caked with white chalk.

Noah peered at his silent classmates. Could the other kids hear his heart knocking in his chest?

"Well?" Mr. Jones asked.

Nothing.

Mr. Jones sighed, turned back to the board, and resumed his chalk-work.

Noah felt his hands shaking on his knees. Then he released the loudest "Quack" his lungs could muster. His classmates seemed to be wrestling between absolute amazement and doing everything they could to hold in their laughter.

Mr. Jones slammed his chalk onto the tray below the board and pivoted to his students. "You've got to be kidding me! Who is doing that?"

The kids stayed silent except for some muffled laughter from Gregg and his buddies who couldn't hold it in any longer.

A knock came from the door. If steam could have risen from Mr. Jones's wig it would have. "We're not finished here." He marched to the door and flung it open.

In the hall stood a woman wearing a *Keep Your Heart in the Heartland* sweatshirt and holding a squirming brown duck.

Thirty seventh-grade jaws dropped.

"Oh, I'm sorry," the woman said. "I'm looking for Ms. Ling's class." She nodded at the duck. "My daughter needs Duck Norris here for show-and-tell."

Mr. Jones hung his head and pointed. "Ms. Ling is across the hall."

"Thanks," she said.

The duck let out a friendly "Quack!"

And the laughter in Noah's Science class sent kids falling from their chairs.

After Science, Noah was nearly carried from the room by a stream of discreet handshakes, subtle slaps on the back, and whispered praise.

"Incredible!"

"That was the funniest thing I've ever seen!"

"You're a legend."

And his personal favorite: "You absolutely have my vote."

He had never been happier in middle school. It's possible he'd never been happier in life. Noah stepped into the crowded hall and his eyes lit up as Katie Frankel hurried from the band room, wearing yellow overalls over a black turtleneck and lugging a French horn half her size. "Check out the flight of the bumblebee!" he yelled.

Everyone turned to Katie and the hallway erupted with laughter. Katie's eyes went wide like a mouse spotted on a kitchen floor and she scurried away from the cackles. A hundred smiles and finger-points came Noah's way. Noah was so happy his face hurt. Gregg gave him a high five and headed to his next class. "Hilarious, Noah." Perry's lips were parted like he had been about to say something, but no words came. His lips twisted in confusion, then he shrugged and chuckled. Down the hall, tiny Katie Frankel seemed smaller than ever when Lucy took her in her arms and ushered her into the safety of the girls' restroom. Lucy glared at Noah and the door shut behind them.

Noah stared at the door. Had he gone too far? Maybe he shouldn't have made the joke. His guilt was interrupted by Samar and Darnell pushing through the wall of giggles. Darnell excitedly put a hand on Noah's shoulder.

"Guess what?" Darnell said.

"What?" Noah asked.

"Gregg swung by Principal Thompson's office before school and dropped out of the election," Samar said.

Noah shook his head. Future had been right again.

"The race is down to you and Claire," Samar said. "You could have an actual shot at winning."

Darnell shrugged. "Maybe even fifty-fifty?"

"Well, depending on how many write-in votes the lunch lady gets," Samar said.

Noah smiled and dreamed of the possibilities. Victory was drifting within his reach. It was so close he could taste it.

Historically, between school bells, Noah rushed to class to get situated for the learning ahead and to avoid any awkward encounters he'd regret later. But for the rest of the day, he enjoyed leisurely strolls through the halls. He exchanged smiles, chuckles, and nods with a dozen classmates who hadn't previously acknowledged his existence. What had typically been one of the more stressful parts of his day had become one of the more pleasant. Why had he ever let it bother him in the first place?

Noah felt so good about his performances in Mr. Jones's class and in the hallway, that he forgot all about the predicament he and Future had gotten themselves into until he shut his bedroom door that afternoon. Future charged from the closet and Noah jumped.

"You scared me!" Noah held a hand to his heart.

"Grab that hundred bucks Grandpa Joe gave us for Christmas," Future said. "We've got some important errands to run before Mom and Dad get home."

Forty-three minutes later Future stepped out from Gary's Discount Printing, a small shop in the middle of a strip mall in the textile district. *Going out of Business Sale* was painted across its window in block letters.

"Got 'em!" Future said, with a smile on his face and a brown paper bag in his hands.

Noah stood with his arms crossed. "I don't understand why we had to use the money Grandpa gave me."

"As opposed to the money he gave me?" Future asked.

Noah shrugged. "We could've at least split it."

"It's literally the same money," Future said. "But I used my version of it on my last trip. Trust me, this was the best hundred dollars you've ever spent."

"I hope so," Noah said. "I was saving for a new bowling ball."

"I know," Future said. "I figure we can ask for one for our birthday. Could you imagine if we had one for the tournament? We definitely would've been able to skip to the finals this week. Come on. That's our ride."

Noah sighed, and the boys hurried through the strip mall's parking lot to a city bus pulling up to the curb. They climbed on, flashed their passes, and sat in the back. The bus lurched forward.

Noah nodded at the paper bag between them. "So?"

"Open it," Future said.

Noah reached inside and pulled out a red T-shirt from a stack of ten. *Vote for Noah* was stenciled across the front in white.

Noah smiled. "Good slogan."

"Feels more clear and to the point, right? Kind of like a walking billboard. Everyone is going to want one after they see Gregg wear it."

"How am I going to get Gregg to wear one of these?"

"You'll figure it out."

Noah's forehead wrinkled. How would he accomplish that? He shot a finger into the air. "Oh! By the way, Gregg dropped out of the race like you said he would."

"Told you," Future said. "How'd you do at school?"

"I think terrific, actually," Noah said. "Big laughs in Jones's class and in the hallway. Definitely getting noticed by some kids who've never given me the time of day. The whole basketball team seems to be coming around."

Future nodded. "Perfect."

"How did everything go with you?" Noah asked.

Future shook his head. "Not great. I don't think I made any progress brainstorming ideas to inspire Mom. I spent most of the day flipping through physics books at the library. They kind of gave me a headache. I was planning to check out as many books as I could and leave them around Mom's stuff in the study, but the librarian told me I couldn't because we never returned that book about African wildlife three years ago."

Noah groaned. "I lost that."

"I know. The photographs were so cool." Future sighed. "Anyway, I did everything I could to convince the librarian to let me check out a couple science books, but she wasn't having it, so I left empty-handed."

"Bummer," Noah said.

Future nodded at the T-shirts in the bag. "You should take the rest of those out of there."

"Why?"

"Because you need to put that bag on your head. Samar's mom is getting on at the next stop."

Noah's eyes went wide. "Seriously?"

"Yeah. You better hurry."

The bus came to a stop and the door opened. Noah frantically shoveled the T-shirts onto the seat and pulled the paper bag over his head. The world went dark.

"Why didn't we just take the next bus from the print

133

shop?" Noah asked. The front of the bag suctioned itself against Noah's lips as he breathed heavily.

"It wasn't going to come for another half hour. Flat tire. And we need to get home before Mom and Dad, or we get grounded and they make us drop out of the race. Don't worry, Samar's mom thinks we're weird anyway."

Samar's mother stepped onto the bus in a skirt suit. She wore her hair in a tight bun and like her son, there wasn't a strand out of place. She blinked at Future and Noah with the bag over his head.

Future raised a hand and elbowed Noah. "Wave," he whispered.

Noah reached up and waved. Samar's mom rolled her eyes and waved back. It seemed she was used to the antics of her son's friends. She took a seat in the front row and stared straight ahead.

"This is so embarrassing," Noah mumbled.

"It's only one more stop," Future said. "Keep your bag on."

Sweat dribbled down Noah's brow and dropped on his crossed arms.

"Couldn't you have run these errands by yourself?" Noah whispered.

Future scoffed. "I mean, I guess? But I didn't want to steal your Christmas money. And I thought it would be nice to spend a little time together. Be a team, you know?"

The paper bag nodded. It had been nice. Mostly. "Sorry, didn't mean to offend you. Just feels risky."

The bus slowed to a stop.

"No offense taken," Future said. "And don't worry, there's nothing to worry about."

Future stood and threw the T-shirts under his arm. He grabbed Noah's sleeve and pulled him to his feet. "Try not to trip on your way out."

Noah stared at his feet through the opening in the paper bag as Future pulled him to the front of the bus.

"Nice seeing you, Mrs. Rao," Future said.

Samar's mother forced a smile. "You too, Noah. Be careful."

"Thanks," said Future and Noah.

She tilted her head and squinted at Noah. Future tugged at Noah's sleeve and Noah blindly followed him down the bus's stairs, taking four big, awkward strides toward the sidewalk. Each step felt like a trust-fall at summer camp. The boys reached the pavement and an air piston fired, pulling the bus's door shut. Noah flinched and the bus drove off.

"You can take it off now," Future said.

Noah removed the paper bag and Future dropped the T-shirts inside. Noah blinked a few times and caught his breath and bearings. They stood in front of a storefront with bridal gowns and three-piece suits on display.

"We crashing a wedding?" Noah asked.

"Just taking one more step toward the best day of your life." Future handed Noah the paper bag. "Hold this. Get on the next bus and ask the driver to wait. I'll be thirty seconds behind you."

Noah returned to his bedroom carrying the paper bag a few minutes after five. Future followed with a long black garment bag draped over his arm. Noah set the T-shirts on his bed and took another look inside. He smiled. "You know, all this stuff for a hundred bucks wasn't a bad deal."

Future cringed. "Well, technically it was a little more than a hundred. I sold the globe at Kimble's Pawnshop this morning."

Noah's eyes went wide. He turned to the desk and noticed his shiny prized possession was missing. "You *sold* it? That was six months' allowance!"

"I know. And we only got a fraction of that from the pawnshop. But you're focused on the wrong thing here. We had an incredibly productive afternoon."

"But it was my globe!"

"*Our* globe. And I'm doing all of this for us. What we're trying to accomplish is way more important than a globe from some catalog, right?"

Noah ran a hand through his hair. "I guess…"

"Look, I risked a lot coming here. And I'm about to spend the next fifteen hours hiding in the closet when Mom and Dad get home, but it'll all be worth it when we're president. Trust me."

Noah exhaled and caught a glimpse of the to-do list on his whiteboard. He shook his head. There was still so much to accomplish. He needed to focus. "You're right. I'm sorry. Thank you."

"It's okay. I know how much the globe meant to us." Future handed Noah the garment bag. "Here."

Noah eyed the bag skeptically. It had a little pink logo that read LENNY'S FORMALWEAR—YOU'LL LOOK ALRIGHT! printed to the right of the zipper running down the middle.

"Open it," Future said.

Noah pulled the zipper to reveal a lime-green tuxedo. He frowned. "Does this glow in the dark?"

"Funny."

"What's it for?"

Future grinned. "School tomorrow."

Noah cringed. "Really? Won't I get in trouble?"

"Why? It doesn't violate the dress code."

Noah shook his head at the tux. "Feels like it should. How come I need to wear this?"

"It'll get more people talking about you."

Noah bit his lip. Had there ever been an uglier shade of green in the history of the world?

"Are you sure I want that?"

Future put a hand on Noah's shoulder. "Haven't you heard the phrase 'There's no such thing as bad publicity'? Everyone in school is going to know your name."

"If I wear this tuxedo?"

"Yeah," Future said. "And if you do one other little thing."

Noah eyed Future skeptically. "*What* other thing?"

14

LUCK OF
THE DRAW...

Two and a Half Days Until the Election

On Tuesday morning, Future rode the bus with a smile. Noah was less happy sitting next to him in his rented lime tuxedo, and more unhappy still with the green paint coating his hands, neck, and face. The other folks on the bus seemed puzzled by Future and his outrageously overdressed green twin. Noah slouched in his seat.

Future patted Noah on the knee. "You don't have to worry about anyone we know seeing us on this bus."

"I don't want strangers to see me either," Noah fumed. "How can this possibly help me earn votes?"

Future shrugged. "You've got school spirit. We're the leprechauns. You're dressed like a leprechaun. It's not hard to understand. This is going to work."

Noah blew hot air through his teeth. "Leprechauns don't have green skin."

Future scrunched his face. "Oh. Maybe well-dressed leprechauns do?" He shook his head. "I think you're taking this too literally. Just focus on the point."

Noah stared at Future. "What is the point?"

"The point is if we want to run our school, people need to know how much we love it. And everyone needs to know who we are."

Noah sighed.

"Do you have the T-shirt?" Future asked.

Noah unzipped his backpack to show a red *Vote for Noah* shirt.

"Excellent."

The bus stopped two blocks from school. Noah took a deep breath, stood, and glanced down at himself. "Is this really going to help?"

"Absolutely. Just one more thing."

"What?" Noah asked.

"Don't take a shot until Larry Gilmore trips."

"Shot at what?"

Future smiled. "You better get going. You're gonna miss your stop."

Noah groaned and trudged off the bus.

"Have a great day!" Future called. "I'll just be busy trying to solve the mysteries of the universe!"

Noah gave a half-hearted wave and sulked down the sidewalk toward the school. On his fifteenth step, a car stuck in the drop-off–line traffic gave a long *HONK!* Noah leapt from the pavement and his heart stopped for a second. He collected himself, took a few steps, and a minivan gave a double beep. The woman behind the wheel called, "That's the spirit, kid!" and someone else shouted, "Looking good!" Noah rolled his shoulders back and marched on.

Noah approached the school and the conversations between his congregating classmates died. All eyes turned his way. He strode up the front steps and gave a friendly nod to Claire Trotter who sat behind a table topped with peanut brittle. Her jaw dropped at Noah's new look. Inside the building, he was met with a hallway of confused faces and whispers, but he soldiered on, offering gracious waves and winks. With nothing to lose, he even dared to shout, "Go Leprechauns!" A few girls on the dance team and Jeremy the janitor responded with seemingly confused applause, just as Noah was broadsided by two shoulders and four arms tackling him into the boys' restroom.

"Ow," Noah said, smothered and sprawled on the checkered tile floor. Luckily, his backpack had broken his fall. Samar and Darnell clumsily climbed to their feet and offered hands to help him up. Noah eyed the outstretched palms. "What was that about?"

"We're saving you," Samar said. "You're in some kind of trouble, right? My mom said she saw you yesterday with a kid wearing a paper bag over his head."

"A bag?" Noah frowned. What to say? "That doesn't sound like someone I'd hang out with."

"Well, that's nice to hear," said Darnell. "But it looks like you're having some kind of...breakdown? You know this isn't a dream, right? That you're actually at school dressed like Kermit the Frog going to prom?"

Noah sighed from the floor, reluctantly took his friends' hands, and allowed them to pull him up. He brushed the creases from his tux while Darnell and Samar watched with concern. He shook his head at their worried faces. "Guys, take it easy. This is all going great. I have a very specific plan. You have to trust me." Noah frowned. Was he sounding like Future? He took a step back and caught a glimpse of himself in the bathroom mirror—green skin and dressed like a butler on Saint Patrick's Day. What had he gotten himself into?

His friends seemed even more concerned.

Samar crossed his arms and rocked on his heels.

Darnell scratched the back of his head. "We're worried about you, Noah. You've been…distant lately?"

Noah nodded. "I know. But it's only temporary while I focus on the election. It's almost over."

"But you look like celery," Samar said.

Darnell nodded. "Or Santa's fanciest elf? What does this even have to do with the election?"

Noah shrugged. "I'm a leprechaun. I've got school spirit."

Darnell and Samar cringed.

"Do leprechauns even dress like that?" Darnell asked.

"They definitely don't have green skin," Samar said.

"That's not the point," Noah said. "The point is people will be talking about me."

Samar sighed. "They'll certainly be talking."

Noah stared at his friends. Was there anything he could say to help them understand? He took a deep breath and shook his head. "I know what I'm doing."

"Are you sure?" Samar asked.

Noah slipped into the hall, leaving his friends to discuss among themselves. He made his way to class and a trail of whispers and frowns followed him. He doubted himself more with each step. His heart pounded. His breathing grew heavy. But the closer he got to Mr. Jones's class, the more the other students' frowns turned into smiles and their whispers into chuckles. Before long, Noah was navigating a sea of uncontrollable laughter and enthusiastic demands for high fives.

"Nice!" Gregg yelled when Noah stepped into Science.

"Legend!" Perry called, and the basketball team cackled their approval. Noah smiled. Mr. Jones rolled his eyes and turned to the blackboard.

Jones spent the period lecturing with his back to the class, while Gregg and Perry referred to Noah as "King Noah." He felt like royalty.

After science, Gregg draped an arm around Noah's shoulder on their way out of the room. "You're hilarious. How come we never hang out?"

"Because you never ask." Noah slapped a hand across his mouth. How could he have said something so uncool? His cheeks turned red. He must've sounded like the most desperate kid in seventh grade to Gregg. But Gregg kept his arm around him and nodded while they strolled down the hall. "Fair enough."

Noah breathed a sigh of relief and the red drifted from his green face. The boys carried on and were greeted by a stream of friendly nods, wide smiles, high fives, an "Alright, Noah!" and several "Go Leprechauns!"

This must be how Gregg felt every day. How Paul once felt. At long last, Noah knew what it was like to be popular at East Hills Middle School. He felt so good that he didn't notice when Gregg drifted away to talk to a few friends from his team. But even without Gregg by his side, the greetings of approval continued. It seemed like his classmates were genuinely happy to see him. And it felt terrific.

When he saw Lucy sitting in math class, she cocked her head and held his gaze for a few seconds, then turned back to the book on her desk. What did her look mean? It definitely wasn't a smile. But any kind of eye contact must be better than none. And in all fairness, he knew he looked absurd.

Ms. Tucker gave Noah a hearty, "Go Leprechauns," and asked him to take a seat. She did her best to keep from smiling throughout class and held him back afterward to see if there was anything Noah wanted to talk about. Darnell and Samar seemed to try to be supportive, but their uneasiness was impossible to hide.

That afternoon, Samar suggested the three of them meet

on the front steps after school, and that's exactly where Noah was heading when he ran into Gregg at the door.

"Nicholson, perfect. We're one short. Let's go." Gregg nodded toward the other end of campus and charged down the hall away from the exit.

"Go where?" Noah asked.

"To play," Gregg called.

Noah frowned and looked outside to see Samar and Darnell waiting for him beyond the doorway. He gave an apologetic shrug and gestured to Gregg. Samar and Darnell gave questioning looks in return. Samar pointed to his watch.

Gregg hollered from farther down the hall. "Come on, Noah."

For a moment, Noah felt rooted to the spot and couldn't do anything but swivel his head from Samar and Darnell to Gregg, then back again. Darnell and Samar were clearly anxious to talk to him about something, but Gregg didn't seem willing to wait. Noah watched Gregg become smaller and smaller, disappearing down the hall. The election was nearly in his grasp and in order to win, he needed Gregg on his side.

Sorry, Noah mouthed to his friends outside, and hurried after Gregg.

Samar and Darnell called after him, but Noah ignored

the twinge of guilt and didn't look back. If he wanted to be president, he had to stay focused.

Noah tailed Gregg, wondering where they could possibly be going. Honestly, the "where" didn't matter. He couldn't believe the two of them had plans together after school at all. After years of keeping his head down and focusing on schoolwork, Noah had finally become appreciated, liked, and respected! Gregg wanted to hang out with *him*.

Noah ran past the school's trophy case, caught his reflection in the glass, and recoiled. He'd forgotten how ridiculous he looked with his green skin and tuxedo. Was Gregg only being nice because Noah looked like a clown? Was that how Gregg saw him?

Gregg pushed his way out the back door and Noah hustled after him to the field behind the school. The grass swayed in the breeze. As usual, a group of students was collecting trash along the chain-link fence. But Noah was surprised to find three dozen kids circled around Gregg and eight other members of the basketball team on the asphalt court, including lanky Larry Gilmore. Most of the popular kids in school were there. And a handful of kids who weren't so popular. The majority of the dance team. A few kids from band. And the twenty or so kids that sat near Gregg's table at lunch.

Noah worked his way through the crowd and up to Gregg. "What is this?"

"Tuesday scrimmage," Gregg said.

"This happens every Tuesday?" Noah asked.

"Only during the school year," Gregg said. "And in August."

Noah took another look at the crowd and the boys on the court. How had he gone through two years of middle school without hearing about the Tuesday game? Noah's concentration was broken by the sound of Perry bouncing a ball on the asphalt.

"Okay, same teams as last time," Perry said. "But Noah's filling in for Max. First to ten baskets. Anything outside the three-point line counts as two. We'll be skins." Perry pulled off his basketball jersey and the T-shirt underneath and four other boys followed suit. It was then that Noah processed he was about to play basketball in front of the most popular kids in school. He felt light-headed.

Perry furrowed his brow at Noah. "You probably don't need to wear the full tuxedo."

Noah glanced down. He'd forgotten about the tux again. His paint-covered hands glistened as he began to sweat. He peeled off his backpack and the green jacket and tossed them behind the nearest basket.

"Game on," Gregg called from mid-court.

Noah turned just in time to see Gregg dribbling straight at him, the other players charging after. Noah leapt out of the way and Gregg smoothly laid the ball up through the hoop, drawing cheers from the crowd and a "Go Gregg!" from Zuri. Noah caught his breath and gave her a wave. It was surprising how invested the spectators were in the game. Before Noah could give it more thought, Perry dribbled past him toward the opposite basket.

"How about some defense?" one of Noah's teammates called. Noah gulped and sprinted toward the ball. Perry planted his feet and launched a perfect jump shot. *Swish!*

"Nice shot, Perry!" yelled Zuri's friend.

Almost immediately Gregg drove the ball to the opposite basket and retook the lead. Then the ball was dribbled to the other basket for a layup by one of Perry's teammates. Noah felt dizzy watching the other nine players run up and down the court. Each team taking turns gaining the lead, then giving it up again.

"Get in the game, Noah!" Gregg yelled.

Noah nodded, but he was thinking about Future's advice. He focused on Larry Gilmore, who was hustling back and forth between the baskets, blocking shots, and making perfect passes to Gregg. Noah had been friends with Larry the summer before third grade when the two of them went to the same day camp. They'd spent countless hours in the pool and playing freeze tag but drifted apart when school started. Noah had no idea Larry was good at basketball. Really good.

"Come on, Noah," Larry called. "Focus!"

Noah ran alongside Larry. What was he was supposed to be doing? And why hadn't he changed out of his dress shoes? His heels hurt and the bottoms of his feet slipped left and right when he jogged forward. It was like wearing cross-country skis or roller skates. Larry passed the ball and Gregg made another perfect shot. The crowd roared.

"One more and we win," Gregg yelled.

Perry shook his head and brought the basketball back into play. And without warning, Larry swooped in and stole the ball. Noah ran alongside him, his dress shoes sliding across the blacktop while Larry dribbled toward midcourt—he had a clear path to the basket! But Noah's right foot slipped a little too far left and went between Larry's legs. Larry tumbled and tossed the ball straight up into the air. Just as Noah offered to help up Larry, the ball arced and dropped into Noah's open hands.

Noah frowned at the basketball. What was it doing between his fingers? And what was he supposed to do about the other team rushing toward him at full speed?

"Do *something*," Larry urged from the asphalt. A shirtless boy lunged for the basketball. In a panic, Noah cocked the ball back with one arm and threw it like a football toward the basket.

"Not that!" Larry yelled.

Noah and the others watched the ball sail through the air from half-court. The ball clanged against the rim, circled the hoop, and fell, shaking the metal chains on its way to the ground. Mouths dropped, hands and fists reached into the air, and everyone jumped for joy! Even the other team!

"That was the craziest shot I've ever seen!" Perry yelled.

"Way to go, Noah!" Gregg shouted, and wrapped an arm around his shoulder. Noah rested a hand on Gregg's back. His heart felt like it was going to explode from the adrenaline and cheers.

Larry clambered to his feet and gave Noah a high five. Then Noah watched Larry's face turn into a frown. "Uh-oh."

Noah followed Larry's gaze. A green handprint sat on Gregg's shirt, squarely between his shoulder blades. It was practically glowing. Noah clenched his lips and peeked at his slimy hands—the paint on his palms was slippery from sweat. "Sorry, Gregg."

Gregg tugged at the back of his shirt to take a look and shrugged. "It's washable, right?"

"Probably?" Noah offered.

"Oh well," Gregg said. "Who cares? Great shot, man."

He frowned at Gregg's shirt. "Thanks, but I feel bad." An idea struck and a grin crept across Noah's face. He raised a finger. "Let me make it up to you."

Noah pushed his way through the crowd leaving the court, getting pats on the shoulder while he hurried to his backpack and jacket. He unzipped the bag, grabbed the red T-shirt, and jogged it over to Gregg. "Here," he said with an outstretched hand. "It's the least I can do."

Gregg cautiously took the shirt and unfolded it. He smiled wide when he saw *Vote for Noah* across the front. "Ha! I'll wear it with pride."

Noah smiled even wider.

After the game, Noah and the basketball team walked to the arcade to play video games and to the Delancey Street Mini-Mart for some Skee-Ball and drinks. The others bought sodas and slushies, but Noah treated himself to a black tea.

The clerk eyed Noah's runny green skin suspiciously and handed him his change. "You okay, kid?"

"Never better," Noah replied.

Gregg chuckled at Noah's drink. "My grandmother

drinks tea. Always tasted like dirty water to me. You actually like it?"

Noah shrugged and the boys made their way to the exit. "It's an acquired taste."

Gregg grabbed the door while the others filed out. "You're a funny guy, Noah. Hey, how'd you know that lady was going to show up in Science with a duck? You pay her or can you just see the future?"

Noah smiled and shrugged. "Quack."

Gregg laughed and slapped him on the back.

The boys said their goodbyes, and the sun moved lower in the sky. Noah strolled home feeling more confident than he'd ever been. He was managing every twist and turn that came his way. Things were going perfectly, and he was on a path to make everything even better. He turned onto his street with a spring in his step but slowed when he saw two figures leaning against the flower box outside his parents' window.

He gingerly moved closer and recognized the figures as Darnell and Samar. They looked furious.

15

NAVIGATING
DESPAIR...

Less Than Two Days Until the Election

Samar crossed his arms and stared down Noah. Darnell wouldn't make eye contact, his focus drifting between the Nicholsons' lawn and their apple tree. Seemingly looking at anything but Noah.

Noah felt like he was going to puke. "I can't believe I forgot about the tournament."

"That makes three of us," Samar said.

"Is there any way we can reschedule?" Noah asked.

Samar shook his head. "After an hour, they made us

forfeit. The Senior Center advanced and already rolled against Eddie's Hardware in the semifinals this afternoon. They're battling Sub Shack in the finals tomorrow."

Noah hung his head. "Ugh. It completely slipped my mind."

"How? We've been looking forward to it all year," Samar said.

"I guess I'm not used to bowling on Tuesdays," Noah said.

Samar exhaled. "Well, if you hadn't tried to roll that fourth strike last week, we wouldn't have had to. What's up with you lately? You've been so—I don't know. Different? Weird? It's like you became a basketball groupie and you don't have time for us anymore."

Noah took a step back. "I've just been super busy with the election. And I'm not a groupie. Those guys are my friends now. I'm sorry I missed our game, but hanging with them this afternoon was really important to the campaign. It was important to me."

Darnell shook his head. "This afternoon was important to us, too. And we also used to be your friends. But that was before you looked like a stalk of asparagus that got stood up at his wedding. This isn't how friends treat each other. Let's go, Samar."

Noah blinked. When was the last time Darnell had

strung together more than one sentence that wasn't a question? And when had he *ever* been mad? "Darnell, I—"

Darnell pushed past Noah and headed to the sidewalk. Samar followed without a word.

"Guys, don't go," Noah said. "That's not what I meant. Guys, wait! I've just got a lot going on."

"Seems like it," Darnell said over his shoulder. "It also seemed like wc used to make time for each other."

"Guys," Noah called, "come back!"

But they didn't.

Noah's lips trembled and his eyes grew wet.

After Samar and Darnell left, Noah shoved his shoes and tux into the garment bag and sulked away to run a bath.

The old claw-foot tub had always been one of his mother's favorite features in the house. She said her grandparents had one exactly like it when she was growing up. Noah hadn't used the tub since he was a little kid, but he didn't have the energy to stand in the shower. How had one of the best days of his life become one of the worst? How could he have forgotten about the tournament? He and his friends had finally earned a real shot at winning, but he hadn't even remembered to show up.

Noah slipped into the bubble-filled tub. His regret remained, but at least the paint began to wash off his hands. He closed his eyes and stewed. The election *was* important. But so were Samar and Darnell. And so was getting Future home—and that didn't seem to be going well at all. Was it possible to feel more overwhelmed?

A knock at the door popped Noah's eyes open. His father poked his head into the bathroom.

"There you are," Dr. Nicholson said. "You're greener than I remembered."

"Hadn't gotten around to scrubbing my face."

"Your brother called to see how you were doing. I think he's been wanting to talk to you."

Noah sighed. What could he even say to Paul this afternoon? *Balancing Pre-Algebra, friends, popularity, a crush, and school politics is impossible?* To Paul it hadn't been. Maybe he could call back in a couple of days after he had it all figured out. He just needed some luck. And time.

"Everything okay, bucko?" his father continued.

Noah stared at the mounds of bubbles coating the bathwater. "Just break-ing more eggs than I'd like recently."

His father leaned against the doorframe. "Bad day?"

"Horrible."

"Sorry, bucko. Someone once told me you need bad days to appreciate the good ones. It may not be the most helpful advice in the moment, but I think it's true. I guess the only other advice I can give is don't forget to circle back to clean up the busted yolks and shells you leave along your way."

Noah stared at his dad. What was he supposed to do with any of that?

"Speaking of eggs," his father continued, "I just used the last of them to cook a frittata and I burned it beyond edibility, so we're cheating and having dinner delivered tonight."

Noah tried to suppress his grin.

Dr. Nicholson laughed. "I can see you smiling."

"I'm not." Noah sank in the tub to hide his lips behind some suds. "What's a frittata?"

"Kind of like a pie-omelet, but usually not as good as either. Don't worry, Gourmet May will be over soon, and I promise your mother and I will never unspool anything so reckless on our tastebuds again. But the good thing is we're trying something outside of our skill sets. And that's something everyone should do every now and then. Don't think we haven't noticed you doing that recently. I know navigating this election stuff has been...*tricky* sometimes. But you're pushing yourself outside of your comfort zone and that's not easy. It takes guts."

Noah's forearms and the back of his neck tingled. "Thanks, Dad."

"But the other thing I need you to know is that it's okay to give yourself a break occasionally. Do you hear me?"

"I hear you."

Dr. Nicholson smiled. "Good. The food should be here in about twenty minutes. Don't forget to wash your face before dinner. We wouldn't want your mom to think you're turning into a turtle." Dr. Nicholson stepped toward the hall and then stepped back. "And bucko?"

"Yeah?"

"Clean your room. That place is becoming a hazmat zone."

Noah felt on-the-way-to-good after finishing his bath and getting a bellyful of dinner. And he felt even better when his mother announced, "You know, I've missed pizza. I can't wait for June so we can go back to doing takeout every night."

An empty grease-stained pizza box sat next to the porcelain figurines of Alice, Dorothy, Peter Pan, and Charlotte in her web. Noah smiled at his father holding his mother's hand on the other side of the dining room table. His mom leaned into his dad's shoulder. He liked seeing his parents happy. And he loved how brilliant they were. They made sense together. His folks weren't only the smartest people on the block, they were two of the brightest minds in the field of physics, and he took pride in knowing there were few problems they couldn't solve.

"Do you think you two could build a time machine?" Noah's eyes went wide. He hadn't planned to ask. The question had snuck from his mouth. It hardly made his parents look up.

"I'm not sure when we'd find the *time*," his mother joked, which made his father chuckle.

"No, seriously," Noah said. "Do you think you could actually make one?"

His parents eyed each other and shrugged.

"Theoretically anything is possible, honey," his mother said.

His father smiled. "I would just worry that if we invented a time machine, that's all anyone would ever want to talk about. Could you imagine how boring that would make our dinner parties?"

His mother giggled.

"But do you really think you could?" Noah asked.

"Could we create a device that transported a person to a different timeline?" his father asked. "Hmm. We've never really thought about it."

Noah's brow furrowed. The hints he'd dropped around the house had been less effective than he hoped.

"There would be some ethical dilemmas we'd need to consider," his father continued. "Would it be morally questionable to allow someone to change the past? Or perhaps gain knowledge from the future? Obviously doing so would have serious implications since those changes wouldn't be made in a vacuum. They'd affect everyone."

"I don't think he's asking us to police it, dear," his mother said with a laugh.

His father tossed a hand in the air. "I'm only saying that when you do something world-altering, it has world-altering implications. Maybe even universe-altering. And those are things that should be discussed."

His mother rolled her eyes. "He's just having fun with the question. He's not serious."

"No," Noah said. "I am serious. This is important. Could you make a time machine?"

Dr. and Dr. Nicholson sat up in their chairs.

"Like, a real time machine?" his father asked.

"Yes."

His parents looked at each other and back to him. His mother smiled gently. "A time machine is probably more science fiction than science fact, honey. I'm not sure we'd even know where to start."

His father nodded in agreement.

Noah slumped in his chair, defeated.

And a few minutes later he slunk off to his room.

The idea of spending the rest of his life hiding in his closet every other night was becoming soul-crushingly real. He sat on his bed by the open window and waited for Future. Maybe together they'd have better luck figuring out a way to get Future home.

The wall clock above the desk ticked along and Noah grew more and more tired. An hour after lights-out, Future still hadn't appeared, so Noah crawled under the covers and waited some more.

He thought about Darnell and Samar. And he thought about Lucy, about the popular kids, and the election. For a moment he thought maybe he should clean his room. Then he thought about how heavy his eyelids were. And eventually he fell asleep.

He sprang from bed early the next morning and found his room still Future-less. He also found a note in his own handwriting on the closet floor:

Had trouble sleeping. Meet me by the
Mini-Mart dumpster before school?

Wear one of the red T-shirts and put the
rest in your bag. You'll need them.

P.S. You should probably do laundry soon.
You're almost out of underwear.

Noah crumpled the note and threw it in the overflowing
bin beneath his desk. He quickly got ready for the day, wearing one of the campaign shirts, and made his way to the
kitchen. He fixed himself a bowl of cereal and spotted the
morning paper next to the emergency landline. It made him
think of Lucy. Was she out there, looking through the same
articles with her mother? He sat at the counter and started
to read.

By the time Dr. Nicholson wandered from her bedroom
into the kitchen, Noah had nearly finished the newspaper, and
the bowl in front of him contained only a tablespoon of sugary
milk. She placed a hand on his head and ruffled his hair on her
way to the dripping coffee machine. "Morning, hon—"

Noah looked up at his mother, frozen in her tracks, staring
down at the paper. She wasn't blinking. He followed her gaze

to a photograph of a windmill beneath a headline that read, *Councilperson Says Sustainable Energy Could Turn Back Clock.*

"Are you okay?" Noah asked.

"Wow." She seemed to be staring through the picture of the windmill. "I just had an epiphany," she said. A smile spread across her face. "That means I—"

"I know what an epiphany is, Mom."

"Oh? Good!" She walked straight past the coffee machine and on to the study. "I've got something I need to work through. You're okay getting to school on your own, right? I think I'm going to need to bounce some ideas off your father this morning."

"Don't you want coffee?"

"I don't need it today," she said, and pulled open the study door and stepped inside.

"Hey, Mom?" Noah called after. "Any chance you just came up with an idea to make a time machine?"

"Maybe, Noah," she responded from the study. "Maybe."

Noah practically skipped to the Mini-Mart parking lot. He found Future leaning against the dumpster, reading a physics textbook. Even from afar, he seemed to have a lot of energy for someone who hadn't slept much the night before.

Future handed Noah a to-go cup without looking up. "I got you a tea. And I finally convinced the librarian to let me check out a book. I still don't have a clue how we're going to inspire Mom and Dad to invent time travel, but I've been learning a bunch about time paradoxes. They're like time problems. Hypothetical situations that someone might experience if they went back in time, like me."

He flipped a page in the book and looked up. At first, Noah couldn't pinpoint why Future seemed so different this morning. But after a moment he understood—Future looked *happy*. And Noah hadn't even told him his great news yet.

"Anyway," Future continued, "it all seems manageable. And as long as you win the election it won't really matter. Life will be great, and we'll just take turns going out into the world every day. Teamwork, you know? We'll look out for each other." Future nodded to the tea he'd handed Noah and gave him a thumbs-up.

Noah chuckled and turned out a palm. "We don't have to worry about any of that! Mom had her epiphany!"

The wind abandoned Future's sails. "She did?"

"You don't seem happy."

Future exhaled and closed the textbook. "No, it's not that. I'm happy. That's great news."

"But?"

"But I was starting to like the idea of staying here with you. Only having to go to school every other day? Problem-solving together? Talking to someone who really understands me? It's been nice. But this is good, too. Are you sure Mom has it figured out?"

"Pretty sure. She saw some article about windmills rotating backward or something?"

Future nodded. "Seems like that could do it."

Noah studied Future. "You're bummed about this, aren't you?"

"Not at all!" Future's cheeks warmed and he examined the concrete. "I think maybe I don't want to get my hopes up?"

"That makes sense."

Future took a sip of tea.

Noah took a sip, too. Tapped his foot and waited for more.

Future took another sip.

"So what did you want to tell me this morning?"

Future squinted at Noah. "Tell you? I just thought it would be nice to hang out."

"Oh."

"You don't think this is nice?"

Noah looked around the cinder-block enclosure, sniffed the dumpster, and forced a smile. "Absolutely nice."

"I don't mean the dumpster. I mean this. Us."

"Right," Noah said. "Yeah. Sorry. It's been great spending time with you lately. Really. I just have a lot on my mind. I mean, you get that better than anyone. And I figured you wanted to tell me what I needed to do today."

"Today?" Future frowned. "You just need to pass out shirts."

Noah glanced down at his red T-shirt. "That's it?"

"Pretty much. And after you give the rest of the shirts away, you'll have kids campaigning for you all over campus. You brought the shirts, right?"

Noah pointed to his backpack. "All set."

"Good. Oh." Future dug into a pocket, pulled out a handful of index cards, and held them out for Noah. "Here. I was going to give these to you tonight, but if you want to get a head start on practicing your speech for the assembly tomorrow…"

Noah's eyebrows lifted and he took the cards. "Wow! You wrote my speech for me? I thought I was going to have to stay up all night doing this." Noah read the first card and chuckled. "It's funny."

"I know."

Noah shuffled through the cards. "This is really cool of you."

"No big deal. And no point in you taking the time to do it after I already have." Future shrugged. "Teamwork."

Noah nodded and stared at one of the cards, loving what he was reading. "This is an awesome speech. I bet everyone went nuts for it, right?"

Future bit his lip. "You'll do great tomorrow. Just read it over a few times so you can make it your own. Because it is."

Noah blushed. "Thank you."

Future put a hand on Noah's shoulder. "Don't worry about it. Also, you should probably number those cards."

"Any chance you have the answers to the math test, too?" Noah asked sheepishly.

Future's eyes bulged. "Are you telling me you haven't been studying? What've you been doing with yourself after school? You know how important this test is, right?"

Noah's mouth dropped open. "No—I mean, yeah. I know. I was planning on studying tonight. But I was also kind of hoping you'd…give me the answers?"

"You thought I traveled back in time carrying the answers to Ms. Tucker's math test?"

Noah cringed. "Yes?"

Future smirked. "Well, then, you're in luck."

"Really?"

"Yes!" Future laughed. "You should have seen your face."

Noah exhaled, relieved. "I'm going to miss having you around."

"I'm going to miss being around. Honestly, I'm a little sad to go. But you'll be okay."

Noah nodded. It *had* been great having Future around. Someone who understood him through and through. "So what's your plan? Mom and Dad don't need much time to build their machine, right? Are you heading back tomorrow morning?"

"We'll see. For now, why don't you just focus on having another great day?"

"Thanks for everything, Future." Noah gave him a soft punch on the arm.

Then Future surprised Noah with a hug. And Noah surprised himself when he realized he needed one.

16

THE HEIGHT
OF FASHION...

The Day Before the Election

As usual, the drop-off line in front of the school was backed up for blocks. Noah felt underdressed in his *Vote for Noah* T-shirt while he navigated the sidewalk past the row of buses and stressed parents attempting to get their kids to school. When was the last time he'd worn a shirt without a collar? Maybe the fourth grade? Other than in PE class, he certainly hadn't ever worn a shirt with his name across the front. It wasn't that he had anything against

T-shirts—wearing one just made him feel unprepared to take learning seriously.

Noah gave a cordial smile and charged by Claire Trotter who stood in the street. Was she directing traffic? And was that traffic moving more efficiently than usual? Noah bounded up the steps while Claire waved a station wagon and an SUV around a big yellow school bus. He shook his head. She must be spiraling.

Noah pulled open the front door and was greeted with a "Nice tee!" from Gregg who shoved a book into his locker. Gregg also wore his *Vote for Noah* shirt! Noah beamed. His wardrobe choice suddenly felt much stronger.

Noah felt a tap on his shoulder and turned to find a curly-haired boy with whom he'd never spoken.

"Hey, um, Noah?" the boy stammered. "Any chance you have another one of those shirts?"

"For me too," said a kid from the marching band.

"We'd take a couple," said Zuri, who stood next to a friend from the dance team.

Noah smiled. He slipped off his backpack and unzipped it, reached inside, and happily passed out red shirts to his classmates who pulled them on over their clothes.

By third period, Noah only had two shirts left and he heard Claire had gone home with allergies. Poor Claire. It was hard not to feel sorry for her. But it was a relief to not have to debate her during lunch. Claire had always been a strong public speaker and argued well. A few years back she somehow managed to convince their class to visit a modern art museum instead of the zoo for their year-end trip because the museum had her favorite kind of orange soda at the snack bar. And that was the year the zoo had a baby gorilla (and the zoo *always* had the best ice cream in the city). It was an impressive feat.

With Claire out of school, Noah only needed to worry about his speech at the assembly and the election the next day. Normally he would have broken out in hives, stressing over what to say, but Future had written such a wonderful speech that Noah wasn't concerned. And it felt great having one thing in life he didn't have to worry about.

While sitting in math, Noah caught Lucy eyeing his shirt. "Hey, no collar," she said.

She'd noticed! But before his lips could form a response, she turned back to the Pre-Algebra book on her desk. He sighed. Why couldn't he have been faster? Darnell and Samar rushed into class just as the bell rang and took the seats closest to the door. Noah waved but couldn't get their attention. Were they still upset?

Ms. Tucker spent the hour standing at the front of the

room talking through the material that would be on the test. But since Noah was getting the answers that evening, he spent the period flipping through Future's index cards, familiarizing himself with the most important talking points and jokes for the speech so they'd sound natural in the assembly. Ms. Tucker glanced over from the board a few times to ask if he was following along, and if he wanted to take notes like the rest of his classmates, but Noah assured her he had it and not to worry.

When the bell rang, Ms. Tucker turned from the whiteboard. "Noah, mind if I see you for a moment?"

Noah sighed and glanced at Samar and Darnell while they gathered their things and left without waiting. He shoved his cards into his pocket, grabbed his bag, and made his way to the front of the room.

Ms. Tucker smiled. "I see you made flash cards for the test. That's good."

"Flash cards?" Noah frowned and shook his head when he realized she was talking about the index cards. "Oh, no. That was my speech for the election."

"Right…" She nodded. "Well, I want you to know I'll be here after school if you want to do a last-minute study session for tomorrow."

"I appreciate the offer, but I think I'm in good shape."

"Are you?"

"Absolu—" Noah caught himself. Was he in good shape? Of course he was! He was getting the test answers from Future. "Yeah. No. I'm good. Thanks anyway, Ms. Tucker. You really are the best. See you tomorrow!"

Ms. Tucker didn't look so sure. "Alright, but I'll be around this afternoon if you change your mind."

Noah was stepping into the hall by the time she finished her sentence.

He found Darnell and Samar whispering at Samar's locker. "Hey, guys, glad I caught you." He dug into his bag. The boys reluctantly turned.

"Wow. Look, Darnell. Noah remembered us," dead-panned Samar.

"We're so lucky," Darnell said.

Noah chuckled uneasily. "Funny." He pulled the last two shirts from his backpack. "I got these for you."

Darnell and Samar stared at the shirts in Noah's out-stretched hand.

"I thought maybe we could all wear them today. Maybe at lunch?" Noah said.

Darnell and Samar continued to stare.

Noah eyed Samar. "Or tomorrow if you don't want to mess up your hair putting it on."

Samar instinctively touched his hair-sprayed head. It remained rock solid.

"I think we'll pass on the shirts," Samar said. "We wouldn't want to give people the wrong idea."

Noah bit his lip and nodded. The words stung. He knew he'd messed up, but did that mean they weren't friends anymore? "Got it. Listen, yesterday was obviously all my fault. I'll admit that."

"It's not just yesterday," Samar said.

"Yeah," Darnell said. "You've barely talked to us all week."

Noah's shoulders grew heavy, weighted with regret. "You're right. I should—"

"Hey, Noah! Got any shirts left?"

Noah, Darnell, and Samar turned down the hall to see Gregg and Perry standing with a few other boys from the basketball team. "Perry needs one," Gregg continued.

"Me too!" said the kid who had repeated sixth grade three times.

Noah glanced at the shirts in his hand and back to Darnell and Samar. The election was so close, and Gregg and his friends could help him win tomorrow.

"Come on, Nicholson," Gregg called. "We have to get to class."

Noah cringed and turned to Samar and Darnell. "Sorry, guys. I'll be just a sec." He hurried down the hall and exchanged his last two shirts for a couple of high fives.

When he returned, Samar and Darnell were gone.

He couldn't find his friends at lunch either. But Gregg invited him to sit with the basketball and dance teams in the cafeteria's center table. Lunch flew by while Noah laughed and listened to the popular kids' stories and jokes and squished down his feelings of guilt. By the end of the day, he felt like the king of middle school again.

In fact, Noah had so much fun he forgot all about his mother's epiphany. When he remembered after the final bell, he nearly sprinted home.

Noah barged into his living room dripping with sweat and found the family's sofa and coffee table off to the side. His parents stood tall in the middle of the room with their sleeves rolled, in front of a time machine.

17

LIKE CLOCKWORK...

Less Than 24 Hours Until the Election

The time machine looked different than Noah had expected. Not less *impressive*—it was a time machine after all—but perhaps less...visually pleasing?

Other than a web of wires running from his father's old laptop, the device basically consisted of the family's long-unused exercise bike and their new blender, both of which sat in the claw-foot bathtub, which had been ripped from the bathroom.

"This is it?" Noah asked.

"You sound underwhelmed," his father said.

Noah squinted at the exercise bike. "It's just not what I was expecting. Is that chewing gum holding those wires in place?"

"It's the perfect adhesive for this kind of thing," his mother said.

Noah peered at the gum and took a whiff. Spearmint. "How does the machine work?"

"How much do you know about tachyons?" his mother asked.

"I've never heard of them," Noah admitted.

His father sighed. "What do they teach you kids at that school?"

"Well," his mother said, "tachyons are tiny particles— even smaller than atoms—that move through our universe faster than the speed of light. Do you know much about Einstein's theory of relativity?"

"I do not," Noah said.

His father shook his head, and his mother continued, "One of the things Einstein theorized was that if something moved faster than light it could reach its destination before it left. Your father and I used that concept to create a machine that could manipulate tachyons to transport something—"

"Or *someone*," boasted his father.

"Back in time," his mother said with pride.

"That's incredible." Noah scratched the back of his head and grimaced.

"But?" his father asked.

Noah took a moment to choose his words carefully. "I guess I thought the machine would look cooler, you know?"

Noah's parents frowned at their son and shrugged at the machine. "I suppose that's fair," his mother said.

"Have you tried it?" Noah asked.

Noah's father proudly pointed at two apples sitting on the coffee table. "What do you think?"

Noah examined the apples. "I think I'm not sure. Are they from our tree?"

Noah's father smiled and put an arm around his shoulder. "Yes, but we only picked one apple this morning. Technically those two apples are the *same* apple."

"Is one of them from the future?" Noah asked.

"Or the past," his mother said. "It's a little complicated to answer at this point. The important thing is the machine works."

"And all because you saw a photo of a windmill in a newspaper?" Noah asked.

"Because I saw a photo of a windmill," his mother confirmed. "It reminded me that tachyons can move in any direction, which got me thinking. And once I wrapped my head around the basic concept, making a machine was surprisingly easy. So presto: time machine. I imagine our conversation with you at dinner had a lot to do with it, too."

Noah grinned at the praise. If only Future was in the room to hear it! Was it silly to want to impress yourself?

Noah examined the simple-looking contraption. It was ingenious, and so were his parents! And now Future could go home. Actually, they could go anywhere. Or was it any-*time*? The possibilities were endless. He smiled at his folks. "This is all great! Now what?"

His father shrugged. "We drag the machine to the garage so it stops throwing off the flow of the living room."

"Then we'll admire it for a few days," his mother said with a smile, "before we dismantle it this weekend."

It felt like the world had come to a screeching halt. Noah took a step back. "Dismantle it? Why?"

"Because of the ethical dilemmas your father mentioned last night," his mother said. "And the possibility that in the wrong hands, this machine could unwind history. Even by someone with the best intentions. A tiny change could alter the lives of everyone on the planet. You see, there's this concept called the butterfly effect. It hypoth—"

"I know what the butterfly effect is," Noah said.

"Great," his mother said. "Then you know why we shouldn't use this machine again."

"It's too much of a risk to even publish our findings," his father said. "I mean, could you imagine if regular people all over the world were building time machines in their backyards? Once you know what to do, they're easier to make than soapbox racers."

"So you're just gonna put it in the garage? Don't you want to send me back in time as another initial test?"

Noah's parents blinked.

"Why in the world would we do that?" his father asked.

"Like if there was something I needed to fix?"

"Sweetie," his mother said, "there's no way we'd let you hurl yourself through time. We love you too much."

His father nodded. "Yeah, bucko, it'd be way too dangerous for you. Not to mention the universe."

Noah's forehead wrinkled. Something wasn't right. Hadn't Future said their parents allowed him to use the machine? Now, with the contraption in front of him, Noah had to admit that it would be out of character for his folks to use him as a guinea pig. Maybe he'd misunderstood Future. Or perhaps things went differently in Future's timeline.

Or maybe Future hadn't been entirely truthful about how he'd gotten here.

Noah's thinking was interrupted when his father began dragging the machine across the carpet.

"Let's just keep this a family secret," his father said. "Honestly, we probably shouldn't have built it in the first place. Sometimes your mother's brilliance blinds our reasoning."

Noah's mother crossed her arms. "Let's not point fingers, honey. We made it together."

"I wasn't pointing fingers. I said *our* reasoning. I'll admit, I was almost as excited as you were."

"Almost?" his mother said. "I could practically see you smiling through your welding mask this morning."

"Fair," his father said. "Completely fair."

Noah stood dumbstruck while his mother helped his

father lug the machine toward the door to the garage. His head spun with questions. How and why had Future actually come into his life? What wasn't Future telling him? And how was he supposed to send him home?

"You should clean your bedroom, sweetie," his mother said. "And start the laundry. You're all out of clothes."

Noah nodded and headed off to review his speech and take a quick nap. He knew he'd have a long night ahead of him memorizing the answers to Ms. Tucker's math test.

Also, he and Future needed to have a serious talk.

18

CONFESSIONS OF
A SEVENTH-GRADE
TIME THIEF...

The Night Before the Election

When Future tiptoed up the family's walkway on Wednesday night, Noah was waiting beneath the cover of the apple tree.

"We should go for a walk," Noah whispered.

Future jumped and threw his hands in the air. "Whoa. Didn't see you there."

Noah pushed past Future to the sidewalk. "Let's go."

Future caught his breath and hurried after Noah. When they'd walked a block from the house he asked, "Everything okay?"

"You tell me, Future." Noah shoved his hands into his hoodie's pockets. "Anything you haven't been honest about? How you got here maybe?"

Future turned up his nose. "What are you implying?"

Noah shrugged. "I'm asking if you lied to me."

"That's a little offensive."

"Well, did you?"

"That kind of accusation is really hurtful." Future shook his head as they wandered down the sidewalk. "I mean, come on, we're on the same team. How can you not trust me after everything we've accomplished? What would I lie to you about?"

"About Mom and Dad allowing you to travel back in time."

"Oh," Future said. "Yeah, *that* I lied about."

Noah ran his hands through his hair. "I knew it! What else aren't you telling me?"

"Nothing!" Future said. "Well, nothing that I wasn't going to tell you tonight."

The boys stopped walking.

Noah squeezed his eyes shut. "Okay. I'm trying to stay calm. You've been a huge help and...I appreciate all you've done for me and the time we've spent together, but what else don't I know?"

"I think we should sit down."

"Just tell me."

Future gestured to the curb. "Sit."

Noah rolled his eyes and sat. Future plopped down next to him. The muffled sounds of a television game show echoed from a house across the street. It was bizarre being upset with his future-self, though Noah had been disappointed with his past-self countless times. Like after he'd eaten two bags of cotton candy at the state fair and paid for it with a vicious stomachache later. He figured this was a similar phenomenon, though Future's betrayal felt worse.

"Talk," Noah said.

"I haven't been entirely honest with you about why I'm here."

"We established that," Noah seethed.

"But I really was going to tell you tonight."

"Okay. So tell me."

Future took a deep breath. "I'm not just here to help you win the election. I'm here to stop you from having the worst day of your life."

"Seriously?" Noah asked.

"Seriously."

"What can be worse than losing my best friends and the election?"

Future dropped his head. "It was a day so awful that if Mom and Dad hadn't invented a time machine, I would have figured out how to make one on my own."

Noah let the news sink in. "That sounds bad."

Future massaged his temples. "It was terrible."

"What happened?"

Future exhaled. "What didn't? First, Ms. Tucker's math test didn't go as well as I had hoped."

"You didn't get a B?"

"I did not." Future dug a hand into his pocket and pulled out a piece of paper folded into a square.

Noah took the paper and unfolded it to reveal a Pre-Algebra test. Beneath the starlight he saw the answers written in his handwriting and the mistakes marked up and corrected with Ms. Tucker's red pen.

Noah looked sick. "You got a fifty-three?"

"*We* got a fifty-three. But you're going to memorize the correct answers on that test so when I get home, we'll have an A."

Noah nodded at the test and did his best to stay calm. But his anxiety was rising. "Okay. I can do that. What happened next?"

"I worked up the nerve to ask Lucy Martinez to the Spring Fling and she said no."

Noah cringed.

"*And* it happened in front of Gregg and Perry," Future continued. "So by the end of my original terrible day everyone heard and was laughing about it."

"Ugh." Noah held his head. "What'd she say?"

"That she didn't know me well enough to go to a dance together."

"But we've gone to school together since second grade."

"That's what I said. And that's what made Gregg and Perry laugh louder."

Noah sighed. His heart pounded. "Alright, well, I think she's gotten to know me much better since you got here."

"I think so, too. And obviously you don't need to ask her to the dance in front of Gregg and Perry."

"Obviously," Noah confirmed. He squinted. "You still think I should ask her?"

"I do. I mean, you two got *tea together*. I never could have done that. Honestly, I think our whole life is in a much better place. We're on a path to get everything we want. I risked a lot coming here. Our goal isn't to avoid having the worst day ever tomorrow, it's to have the best."

"The best," Noah repeated with a nod. "Alright, what else? I already know you lost the election. How? The speech is amazing."

"Thanks. I didn't have a chance to give it."

Noah's head snapped back. "How come?"

"My pants ripped in front of the whole school."

Noah went pale. "What?"

"When I got called to the podium during the assembly. They had us sit on the stage and somehow my pants got stuck to one of those little round bolts that connects the top of the chair to the legs. The back of my pants tore right open."

Noah's jaw dropped.

Future pursed his lips. "It gets worse."

"Worse than the whole school seeing my underwear?"

"Yeah," Future said with a solemn nod. "They were pink."

Noah's eyes went wide. "Pink underwear?" He ran a hand through his hair. "I mean, there's nothing wrong with that...."

It's just a color, right? Who cares? But I, uh, don't even own pink underwear."

Future put a hand on Noah's shoulder. "Noah, it's me. We got a pair of pink underwear in that multipack from Grandma for Christmas. They're in the back of the drawer."

"Well, yeah, but we would never wear them."

"We did tomorrow."

"Why?"

"Because they were the only clean pair left."

Noah stared wide-eyed at the street. "I should probably throw them away and do a load of laundry."

"That's what I was thinking, too."

The boys sat in silence.

Noah bit his lip. "Does anything else go horribly wrong tomorrow?"

Future shook his head. "That's it. But if we can't change the past we're going to have to deal with the consequences in the future."

Noah rubbed his forehead. "Okay. This all feels manageable."

"Yep. It's what we've been preparing for since I got here."

"Totally," Noah said. He tried to convince himself that it was true, and that they had everything under control. But why didn't it sit right? "Can I ask you one thing?"

"Sure."

"Why did you wait until tonight to tell me all of this?"

"We don't handle pressure well, Noah. I didn't want to stress you out. We're worriers."

Noah nodded, feeling a stew of troubled thoughts swirl in his belly. "True."

"I needed you to focus on our goals for each day instead of spending a week and a half freaking out about tomorrow. We never would've accomplished everything you have if you had it all hanging over your head."

"Makes sense." It was hard to disagree.

They glanced up when a wood-paneled station wagon pulled to a stop in front of the curb. The driver-side window rolled down and an older woman wearing purple curlers poked her head out. "You two okay?"

Future shrugged. "Time will tell."

"Huh?" said the woman.

"Thanks for checking, ma'am," Noah said. "We'll be fine."

The woman gave an uneasy nod and lifted her foot from the brake.

"Hopefully," Noah called as the woman rolled away down the road.

19

FINAL PREP...

14 Hours Until the Election

The boys crept through their bedroom window and went straight to the dresser. Noah grabbed his last pair of clean underwear and threw them into the trash. Future gave a supportive nod to Noah and a shake of the head to the pink briefs in the wastebasket.

Noah eyed the dirty clothes on the floor and the overflowing hamper. "I'll start a load of laundry first thing."

"Sounds like a plan," Future said. "Mind if I take the bed?"

Noah blinked. "Really?"

"You're going to be up all night studying anyway."

Noah sighed and pulled Ms. Tucker's test from his pocket. "Take the bed...."

"Appreciate it." Future kicked off his shoes and climbed under the covers.

Noah sat at his desk, smoothed the creases on the exam, and began painstakingly and methodically memorizing it, one problem at a time. It was like trying to memorize a page from a book written in a foreign language. Why hadn't he paid more attention in math that week? And would Future stop snoring so he could concentrate?

Noah didn't have a clue how to solve any of the seventeen problems on the test. But his eyes became bloodshot drilling each answer into his mind. He'd be able to "show his work," he just wouldn't be able tell anyone what any of that work meant. As the night went on, he became more and more impressed that Future had been able to score a fifty-three. He must have worked hard. And he must have been devastated to discover his hard work had still resulted in a failing grade.

By the time Noah felt sure he knew the seventeen problems backward and forward, he was too exhausted to drag himself to the closet, so he rested his head on the desk and closed his eyes. It seemed like five minutes later that he bolted upright in his chair when the bedroom door shut.

"Morning," Future whispered, carrying a warm mug of black tea.

Noah gathered his bearings. The sun was rising, and his floor was still covered with clothes. And he slowly realized he couldn't see out of his left eye. He shook his head in a panic and banged a hand against his right ear.

"Let me help you." Future reached down and peeled the math test off Noah's face.

"Ah," Noah said. "Better."

Future frowned at the paper. "Looks like you drooled a little. Kind of tough to read the answers on a couple of these."

Noah blushed. "It's okay. I got it all memorized." He tapped his head and blinked a few times, still trying to wake up. Had he ever been so tired?

"Excellent. Here. I made this for you." Future handed Noah the tea.

Noah smiled and took a sip. "Just what I needed."

"You should get the wash going," Future said.

Noah nodded, sat the mug on the desk, and stood. His body was sore from sleeping upright. He stumbled to his laundry bin and stomped down on it to make room. He tossed as many pieces of clothing into it as he could. Then he scooped up his *Vote for Noah* T-shirt and dropped it on top.

"You're going to do great today," Future said.

"You think?"

"I know." Future eyed the window. "I should get out of here before Mom and Dad wake up."

"Will I see you again?"

Future grabbed his backpack from the closet and slung it over a shoulder. "Depends how today goes. So probably not."

"Oh." Noah eyed the carpet. "I'm, um—I guess you leaving kind of snuck up on me. I don't really know what to— well, thanks, and—"

Future waved off Noah's stumbling reply. "Hey, don't get too sentimental. You're about to have the best day of your life. But you've got work to do and you need to stay focused. You can do all of it."

Noah smiled and Future pulled him in for a hug. "Just be us, Noah, and we'll be fine."

Noah nodded, lifted the window, and helped Future down.

"If Mom and Dad ever rebuild their machine, maybe you can visit sometime," Noah whispered.

"Maybe you visit me?"

Noah chuckled and exchanged waves with himself.

After Future slipped away, Noah started the washing machine, sat on his bed, and finished his tea. But the caffeine didn't kick in right away, so moments after his last sip he passed out again. Sometime later he was shaken awake by his mother.

196

"You should hop in the shower, sweetie. School starts in fifteen minutes. I can give you a ride."

Noah's eyes bulged and he jumped out of bed.

"Up late studying?" she asked.

"Yep," he said, and hurried into the hall. "Math test."

"Good boy. I put your laundry in the dryer."

"Thanks, Mom!" he called, and went to rinse off.

Noah took the fastest shower of his life, wrapped himself in a towel, and rushed to the dryer. He pulled open the door and glared. Something wasn't right. "Are all of these clothes mine?" he shouted.

"Not sure who else they'd belong to," his mother responded.

Noah reached into the dryer, hauled out two armfuls of clean laundry and placed them on top of the machine. He stared in horror. His socks, undershirts, and underwear had become a vibrant shade of pink. He shuffled through the mound of clothes with his jaw hanging. All of his once-white underwear had become pink, pink, pink. But how? He reached into the pile and pulled out his red *Vote for Noah* T-shirt. Never had a piece of clothing looked so guilty.

"We should get in the car, sweetie!" his mother called from the kitchen.

Noah stood frozen.

His mom poked her head into the laundry room. "You're

going to be late. We need—" She frowned at the laundry. "What happened to your clothes?"

Noah held up the red shirt.

"Oh," she said. "I can't believe I didn't notice earlier. Must have been in a rush. Well, don't worry, it's not like anyone is going to see your underwear."

He wished with all his heart she was right. It wasn't feeling like the best way to start the day.

While his mother went in search of her keys, Noah reluctantly stepped into a pair of pink boxer shorts and tucked a blue collared shirt into his freshly washed khakis. Luckily the tan pants hadn't turned pink. It hurt not being able to do some (supervised) ironing first—he'd have to live with a few wrinkles. It made his skin crawl. Being wrinkle-free was typically one of the few things he could control in life, but today there was no time. There wasn't time for breakfast either, so on the way to the car Noah grabbed one of the two apples from the coffee table.

Noah's mother pulled into the long drop-off line and they came to a standstill. She and Noah eyed the clock on the dashboard. "You're going to be late," she said. "Better walk from here."

Noah groaned at the traffic and reached for the door handle.

"Oh!" she said. "I almost forgot. Paul called again yesterday when he was running into his last final. He said you never called him back? But he wanted me to tell you to just have fun with your speech and not to sweat it too much if things don't go perfectly."

Noah forced a smile. How was that helpful? He pulled the handle and hopped out. "Thanks for the ride, Mom." He shut the door and turned on a heel.

"Hey, sweetie?"

Noah looked back through the open passenger window.

"You're going to do great," she continued. "You've worked hard. Now everything is just up to the wills of the universe."

Noah nodded at his mother and hoped the universe was on his side.

He bit into his nearly finished apple and headed to school, exchanging hellos and waves with the other kids hurrying toward the building.

"Good luck!" said the boy who never showed up to English class.

"Thanks!" Noah said, and charged the front steps. He took a final bite from the apple and tossed it toward a metal garbage can. But when he released the core, a butterfly caught his eye. Noah watched the little purple wings flutter up past the East Hills Middle School sign and over the school, not noticing the apple core bounce off the can's rim and down the steps.

Noah pulled open the front door and stepped inside to face the day.

20

BUCKLE UP FOR TURBULENCE...

Election Day

Perry clapped when Noah strolled into Mr. Jones's Science class.

"There he is, folks," Gregg announced. "Our future class president. Don't forget to vote for Noah this afternoon."

Noah chuckled and bowed, which made the basketball team laugh. He took his seat, nodded at his cheering classmates, and felt his chances jump from good to great. He really could win this. He and Future had worked hard, and today everything they'd worked toward would come to be. Today could be the best day of his life.

While Mr. Jones lectured about plants turning sunlight into energy through the wonders of photosynthesis, Noah shuffled through his index cards. He wanted to keep Future's speech fresh, but he already knew it so well that he didn't need the cards. Mostly he wanted to avoid thinking about his underwear. But whenever Noah tried to not think about something, it usually made him think about that thing more. His mind played an endless loop of his pants ripping onstage in front of the entire school. He was going to have to avoid the chair Future had sat on during the assembly. But how would he know which chair that was? He'd figure something out. He had to.

After class, Noah moseyed into the hall to find Gregg and Perry already talking to Zuri and the rest of the dance team.

"Maybe wear a blue shirt," Zuri told Gregg. "My older sister has a pair of blue pants that I've been dying to borrow."

Noah looked between Gregg and Zuri, trying to make sense of the conversation. Gregg clocked his confusion. "Zuri and I are going to the Spring Fling."

"Oh!" Noah said. "That's awesome." He was surprised by how happy the news made him. Zuri was nice.

Perry smiled at one of Zuri's friends from the dance team. She smiled back.

"Who are you going with, Noah?" Gregg asked.

"Me?" Noah bit his lip. "I'm probably not going."

"But you have to," Perry said.

"Yeah, Noah. Everyone expects you to be there," Zuri said.

Noah frowned. It was strange imagining the popular kids would ever expect him to be anywhere. His frown turned into a grin.

Gregg gave Noah a playful slap on the back. "We see you smiling. Who are you thinking about taking?"

"Lucy Martinez." Noah winced. The name had left his lips without thinking. A reflex. It was true, obviously, but did he want anyone else to know? He looked to Gregg, Perry, and Zuri to see what they thought.

Zuri nodded. "She's cool."

"Yeah," Perry said. "I've got English with her. She always gets the best grades in class on her essays."

"Hey, there she is," Gregg said.

Noah followed Gregg's outstretched finger to Lucy, who was fiddling with her locker less than twenty feet away. She wore her sweater with a mockingbird knitted across the front. "You should go ask her," Gregg continued.

Noah's cheeks grew warm. "I don't know...."

"Better hurry," Perry said. "Before someone else does."

"Or she asks someone herself," Zuri said.

Noah stared at Lucy. Gregg, Perry, and Zuri stared at him.

He tapped a finger against his brow. "You really think I should?"

"Absolutely," Gregg said.

"Go," Perry said.

"No time like the present," Zuri said.

Noah's shoulders dropped under the weight of their expectant eyes. How could he say no to them? But wasn't this where things first went wrong for Future? Then again, he was light-years ahead of where Future had been. Perhaps *this* was the moment when Noah's worst day would begin to become his best. He took a deep breath and walked toward Lucy.

"Attaboy," Gregg said.

"You got this," Zuri called.

The thirteen steps Noah took crossing the hall felt like thirteen miles. He could almost feel the others staring at the back of his head. What should he say? What *shouldn't* he say? How had Future fumbled things in the past? (Or was it in the future?) He arrived at Lucy's locker and drew a blank, and she flung open the door into his nose. *Bang!*

Lucy, Gregg, Perry, and Zuri cringed. Noah's hands shot over his face. "Ow." He did a quick feel to make sure his nose wasn't broken or bleeding. And everyone in the hall turned to watch him and Lucy.

"Sorry," Lucy said through her teeth, grimacing. "I didn't see you."

"It's okay," he said. "My fault."

"You're really okay?" she asked.

Noah pulled his hands from his face and slipped them into his pockets. "I'm fine."

They eyed each other awkwardly.

"So...hi," he said.

"...Hi."

What was he supposed to say next? Should he just come out with it? He swallowed. "Would you like to go to the dance with me?"

The question hung. Someone in the hallway gasped. And it didn't appear anyone was breathing.

"Really?" she asked.

"Well, um, yeah."

"Oh," she said. "No."

Noah blinked.

Gregg, Perry, and Zuri looked away. Everyone else in the hall seemed to anxiously await what Noah would do next.

Mortification overtook Noah's body. "I—" But he didn't know what he was or what to do, and his insides were doing backflips. So he left Lucy at her locker and hurried down the hall. No one laughed or spoke while he made his exit. The only things Noah heard were his shoes on the linoleum and his heartbeat echoing in his chest.

He pushed his way into the boys' restroom and locked himself in the middle stall. He leaned against the green wall, waiting for his heartbeat and breathing to return to normal.

Why did he have to crash and burn in front of so many people? More importantly, did he feel bad because he regretted asking her, or was he simply disappointed she had said no? Oddly, the question made him feel better—because he wasn't sure.

Noah took a deep breath. He couldn't let one major setback sink the whole day. There was still an election to win, an exam to ace, and an all-time-great day to be had.

Noah shook his head and pulled his drool-stained math test from his pocket. He studied until the bell rang at the end of second period. Then he studied a little more.

Noah wandered from the boys' restroom just in time to run into Lucy outside Ms. Tucker's classroom. His heart sank. They stopped shoulder to shoulder at the open door. Lucy seemed as uncomfortable as he was. She looked away and adjusted the hair tie holding her ponytail. Noah examined his shoes. He swallowed and stuck out a hand, offering to let her go first.

"Please," Lucy said, and shook her head. "I insist."

"Thanks," Noah mumbled. He walked into the room trailed by Lucy.

Gregg caught his eye and offered a sympathetic what-can-you-do shrug as Noah took his seat. The whiteboard was covered with fifteen Pre-Algebra problems that Noah couldn't make heads or tails of. A concern for another day. He reached into his backpack and grabbed a pencil. Samar and Darnell were hunched over their textbooks, cramming in some last-minute studying.

"Good luck, guys," Noah said.

Samar rolled his eyes and Darnell offered a toothless smile.

"Oh no," Lucy said, looking at Ms. Tucker. Ms. Tucker sat at her desk with a Band-Aid on her forehead and a dirt stain on the sleeve of her blouse. "What happened?"

"Just a tiny scratch," Ms. Tucker said with a sigh. "I was running late and I slipped on an apple core in front of the building."

Noah's mouth dropped open. Somehow he knew the apple was his. He felt a cramp forming in his stomach.

"Have you ever heard of such a thing?" Ms. Tucker continued. "Banana peel, sure. But apple core? Leave it to me.... But I'm fine. The biggest casualty was your test. I had it in a manila folder so I could make copies in the office, but when I slipped the folder went flying and the test got caught under a bus leaving the drop-off line."

Ms. Tucker got up and walked toward the board. "Anyway, I was in a hurry to find a bandage, so I didn't have time to type up the questions. Apologies everyone, you'll have to use your own paper." She tapped a finger on the whiteboard. "I've got a few extra sheets if anyone needs some. As always, no talking. And no calculators. You've got until the bell."

Noah's classmates pulled out notebook paper and dove

into the exam. He stared at the board and the room spun. Noah shot a hand into the air.

"Yes, Noah?" Ms. Tucker asked.

"Are these the same questions from the test you lost?" he asked, knowing the answer.

"Um, no," she said, looking at Noah slightly suspiciously. "I guess the original questions are either lost forever at the bus depot or blowing down Main Street. I hate to litter, but unfortunately sometimes it's unavoidable. Anyway, I assure you, these questions are just as good, if not better."

She smiled, took a seat, and began reading a book. Noah felt sick.

He glared at the board trying to decode what any of the problems were even asking. But the letters, numbers, brackets, and fractions didn't make any sense. Where should he even start? He wasn't sure, so he didn't. He only sat and sweated, listening to his classmates' pencils work through the exam.

Eventually Darnell got up, placed his test on Ms. Tucker's desk, and returned to his seat to quietly read. Samar followed shortly after. And one by one, the rest of Noah's classmates did the same. Noah placed his head on his desk and tried not to cry.

When the bell rang, Ms. Tucker glanced up from her

book. "Have fun at the assembly, everyone. Break a leg, Noah." She held a finger to her chin. "Wait, Noah, did you turn in your test?"

As the other kids collected their things, Noah grabbed his bag and dashed from the room.

He ran right back to his middle stall and threw up.

21

ASK NOT WHAT YOUR SCHOOL CAN DO FOR YOU...

One Hour Until the Vote

The auditorium buzzed with conversations and laughter. The room was nearly full by the time Noah made his way to the front. He had been gargling sink water to get the taste of vomit out of his mouth and had done a decent job all things considered.

"There you are," Principal Thompson called from the stage. He tightened his purple tie. "Get up here and sit."

Two rows of chairs had been lined to Thompson's right. In the first, Claire Trotter sat between two empty seats.

The second row had the school's choir. Lucy and her friend Maria sat in the middle.

Lucy meekly raised a hand at Noah. He nodded at her and eyed the seats next to Claire with dread. Which chair would lead to certain doom? They looked identical, neither more sinister than the other, so he wasn't sure. He still felt queasy from the math test and his disastrous rejection, and the idea of ripping his pants and becoming the laughing-stock of his class was more than he could handle. Especially after all he'd done for his campaign.

"I can't," Noah said.

Principal Thompson frowned. "Can't what?"

"Can't sit on the stage, sir."

Principal Thompson shook his head. "Sure you can. We're starting in a few minutes."

Noah took a deep breath. "No, sir. I'm sorry. I can't."

Claire scratched her head and discreetly smelled her armpit. Lucy's eyebrows rose.

"I don't understand," Principal Thompson said. "Are you dropping out? First Gregg, now you. Kids these days...We can't even hold a proper election."

"I'm not dropping out, sir. I'm just not comfortable sitting on that stage. I'm—" Noah glanced at the ceiling. Maybe there would be an explanation up there? A smile flashed across his face. He turned to the principal. "It's just that if I'm going to represent my fellow classmates, it's important that I remain one with them. I want to be their elected official. Their friend and supporter. Not lording over them like middle school *tyrant*."

A few kids sitting toward the front of the auditorium nodded and clapped their approval.

Claire sank in her chair.

Principal Thompson's eyes narrowed at Noah. "Are you serious?"

"Completely."

Principal Thompson shrugged. "Fine. Stay close."

"Thank you, sir." Noah slipped into one of the green-cushioned theater seats with the crowd. He felt his fingers sweat.

"Let's go, Noah!" Gregg called from the back of the auditorium.

"Yeah Noah!" Perry yelled, which ignited applause from the room and an eye roll from Principal Thompson.

Noah gave a smile to the basketball team and wiped the sweat from his hands onto his pants. His leg bounced and his nerves got the best of him. He put a hand on his knee to control his restlessness and saw the wrinkle on his thigh. Oh, that. Ugh…He tried to smooth out the crease, but it was useless. The longer Noah glared at the wrinkle, the more his leg itched. And the more he itched, the more his mind wandered. How could he stop the nightmare scenarios from running through his head? He pulled the index cards from his pocket for a final read-through and was reminded what a tremendous speech Future had written. He was so engrossed in Future's words that he didn't notice the assembly had begun.

Startled, he bumped his funny bone on the chair while the choir sang the school's fight song at the front of the stage. *Ow.* He winced and peered up. His elbow tingled.

> *"We are the Leprechauns of East Hills,*
> *Excellence in academics is what our school*
>   *instills.*
> *On the fields and the courts our athletes are*
>   *plucky,*
> *And we're not shy to boast that we're also*
>   *lucky. . . ."*

Noah massaged the strange sensation from his forearm and listened to Lucy sing with the choir. His eyes twinkled. Was she was singing directly to him? Suddenly, he was less concerned about failing his math test and being turned down for the dance. All he cared about was her beautiful voice. It was soothing. He was ready to give Future's perfect speech. Maybe everything else had gone wrong, but the election was in the bag and the universe was finally on his side.

Noah stared up at Lucy. She winked down at him. Noah blinked. What did the wink mean? Maybe she didn't completely hate him. His lips parted and the song came to an end:

> *"Cheer on the Green and wear it with pride,*
> *Our spirit and character cannot be denied!"*

The choir took a bow to polite applause—Noah clapped the loudest—and filed into the row of chairs behind Claire and Principal Thompson.

"Vote for Noah!" yelled someone in the crowd.

"Go Noah!" shouted another kid, followed by a "Yeah!" and hearty approval from the basketball and dance teams and everyone sitting around them.

Noah looked over his shoulder and gave a confident wave.

Principal Thompson shook his head. He approached the podium and tapped the microphone. "Quiet, please. The only campaigning in this room should be done by the candidates during their time to speak. Let's show respect for both our nominees. Claire and Noah have put in a tremendous amount of work. We should be proud of the way they represented themselves and this school throughout their campaigns. This has been a fair and honest election."

Noah slouched in his seat and eyed Claire. She had her hands folded in her lap and her attention politely focused on the principal.

"Well, okay then," Thompson continued. "Thanks to the show choir for another spirited performance." He gave a cordial nod to the choir. "I suppose we should get on with it. Without further ado, your first candidate for class president, Noah Nicholson."

Gregg and his friends leapt from their seats to cheer, which prompted the rest of the room to stomp their feet and slam their hands together in excitement. Noah closed his eyes, feeling the room shake, and took a deep breath. Could anything sound more fantastic than shouts and applause for him? The election was his. He'd follow in his older brother's footsteps. A family middle school political dynasty. Noah and Future had rewritten the history of the universe. Well, at least the history of East Hills' seventh-grade politics.

As Noah stood and stepped toward the stage, he felt a tug at his side, like one of his enthusiastic supporters was pulling him back. He tried to take another step. Had a classmate's hand slipped into his pocket? He attempted to move a third time and glanced down to find that the corner of his chair had caught in his pocket. But by the time he processed what he was seeing, it was too late. The chair ripped the backside of his khakis, from one pocket to the other.

Oh. No.

For a moment, there was less oxygen in the room while the entire audience gasped at Noah's pink underwear. Noah tried to hold the back of his pants together and the auditorium exploded with laughter. Flustered, he turned his backside from the crowd, only to realize he was displaying his underwear to his principal and classmates on the stage. Lucy's mouth hung open while Maria giggled next to her. Noah turned burgundy.

So much for a family dynasty.

The longer Noah stared in horror at the snickering faces, the more he worried he really would lose to write-in votes for the lunch lady.

He ran for the exit, drenched in embarrassment and an unshakable feeling of déjà vu. The door closed behind him. But he could still hear the laughter.

22

DOUBLE TROUBLE...

Thirty-Three Minutes Until the Vote

Noah didn't stop running until he reached his front door. He grabbed the hide-a-key beneath the little stone gargoyle beside the mat and stumbled inside. His folks were at work, so the house was dark, which was ideal since he felt like hiding at the bottom of a well. Echoes of laughter rang in his head.

He wandered down the hall to run himself a bath, but when he entered the bathroom, he found an empty space between the shower and the sink.

"The tub's still part of the time machine…." he muttered to himself.

He hung his head, went to his room, and swapped his torn khakis for a pair of pajama bottoms from the floor. Now what? Maybe he should watch TV? Anything to avoid thinking of the catastrophe he'd made of his school and social life.

Noah headed toward the living room couch and something caught his eye: a purple Coconut Chaos wrapper on the kitchen counter.

He picked it up. "Future?"

"In here."

Noah followed the voice to the garage, where Future sat on the exercise bike in the bathtub. He was eating another candy bar.

"Feels like a bad sign that you're home during school hours," Future said. "Should I be reading into the fact that you're wearing dirty PJs instead of pants, too?"

Noah rubbed his eyes. "It all went wrong. Everything. The test, Lucy, the election. Just…bad. We failed."

Future shrugged nonchalantly. "Oh well. You tried." He took a final bite from his Coconut Chaos bar and dropped the wrapper into the tub.

Noah frowned. "You're taking this really well."

"I knew it might not work. It didn't the first seventeen times I went back either."

Noah went pale. Future had lied to him. *Again.* "This is the *eighteenth time* this has happened?"

"Nineteenth if you count my original attempt." Future sighed.

"You said you went back in time twice before this."

"I did go back twice," Future said. "But I went fifteen other times, too. Feels like I'm getting closer every trip, but I knew you'd probably fail. Still got a few wrinkles to iron out."

Noah clenched his hands into fists. "You sent me out to fail?"

"Not to fail. I hoped you'd get lucky."

Noah took a deep breath. Would the neighbors hear if he screamed? "I can't believe you put me through that!"

"Put *you* through that? Do you have any idea how much I've invested in this? How much stress I've put myself through? I did all of this for us. And you would've done some version of it on your own anyway. Just, you know, worse."

"But you could've told me we wouldn't succeed! I could have done everything differently. You could have said to forget the election. Not worry about Lucy and just spend the week studying for the math test."

"You wouldn't have listened to me. Mom, Dad, and Ms. Tucker all told you that and you didn't care. You're just like me—you were determined. You wanted everyone to know you're just as good as Paul. I only provided guidance and encouragement."

"You encouraged me to ruin my life."

"That's a bit harsh. I was trying to help you make our life better."

"You were trying to make *your* life better. Without caring what would happen to me if your plan didn't work."

Future held up a hand. "Whoa. Take it easy. Eventually I'm going to get all of this figured out and we'll both get what we want. You're acting like I'm the bad guy."

"Oh, come on, Future. You know it was selfish of you to put me through all of that."

Future laughed. "*I'm* selfish? We're literally the same person."

Noah shook his head. "Not anymore. I'm better than I was a week and a half ago."

"Better? No. Be real, Noah. Maybe I'm a little more jaded after living through nineteen disastrous election days. And maybe you've had different experiences. And maybe for a moment you were more popular. But you're still self-centered."

"*Me?*" Noah crossed his arms.

"Yeah, *you*. I mean, think about your anxiety—when was the last time you got nervous, or worried because you were thinking about somebody else? You get stressed out fixating on yourself. You abandoned Samar and Darnell, and it hasn't even occurred to you to actually apologize. You haven't called Paul back even though he's checked on you twice. Mom and Dad have been asking us to clean our room for weeks, and you've done *one* load of laundry and only because you absolutely had to. You've been trying to get Lucy Martinez to go out with you forever because it would be good for you, but you barely know anything about Lucy. What does she like to do for fun on weekends? What are her hobbies? Her favorite books and TV shows? You don't have a clue. And don't even get me started on this election. I mean, we cheated! You had no problem taking my speech or the guidance I gave you to navigate the last week and a half. And we still *failed*, but you were willing to cheat on your campaign by manipulating people through time travel just as easily as you were willing to take the answers for Ms. Tucker's math test. You didn't give any of it a second thought."

Noah threw his hands in the air. "You're being so unfair! I was only doing what you told me. I trusted you. You were the one who said this would be the worst day of my life. And come on, you know more than anyone how important being class president is to me—to us."

"I know," Future said. "And that's how I *really* know you're selfish, Noah. *Why* do we want to be class president? It's not for the school. All I want—all *we* want—is to be as good as Paul. For Mom and Dad to respect us as much as they respect him. We're desperate for our parents to trust us to do things without them hovering. And I know all of that *because* you're me. Maybe the world doesn't revolve around us, but sometimes we wish it did and that's why we put ourselves first even when we know we shouldn't. We're selfish, Noah. We're the same."

Noah felt dizzy. He crouched and sat cross-legged on the concrete. The words stung. Especially because they were true. "Well…well, maybe I don't want to be the same anymore."

"Are you saying that to me or yourself?" Future asked. "I guess it doesn't really matter." He hopped off the bike and approached Noah. "Listen, I know you've been through a lot, but there's good news for us."

Noah looked up hopefully.

Future gave Noah's shoulder a squeeze. "You don't have to worry about school tomorrow or anything that went wrong today."

Noah dropped his head into his hands. "Ugh. I hadn't even thought about tomorrow."

"Well, don't."

Noah frowned. "What do you mean?"

"Every time I've gone back, I've left a few minutes earlier than the previous trip so I can convince my past-self I can take it from there. I send them home to wait for me to get everything right. That's why there aren't seventeen more versions of us in this garage. But the last couple of days I've been thinking. And I'm pretty sure I've been going about this the wrong way."

"*Clearly*," Noah said.

Future shook his head. "Listen, when you came to see

me at the library the other day and we talked at the koi pond that was the first time we had that conversation. Because this has been the only time we've had trouble breaking the blender, right?"

"That wasn't my fault, Future. And we worked together to solve it."

"I know," Future said. "I'm not pointing fingers, I promise. My point is that conversation was the best I've felt since this whole thing started. And it was because we understand each other in ways no one else can. These trips have been lonely. *Life* can be lonely. Even when you're surrounded by other people. But that loneliness goes away when you find someone who really gets you. And who gets us more than us?"

Noah thought back to all that they'd done in just a few days. Their conversation about hopes and fears. Their late-night whispered chats to plan their days ahead or morning talks over tea. Even their adventure picking up the printed shirts. Future made a strong point.

"What we're trying to achieve is hard, but it's not impossible," Future continued. "Through trial and error, we can eliminate all the paths that don't work until only the correct path is left. Let's go back together. Start over. If two heads are better than one, then three heads are better than two. We can figure this out as a team. Be ready for anything. Be like those librarians with their beach towels and clean up this mess. And honestly, I could use a friend. Come back in time with me."

Noah's jaw hung. "Wow." He stared at Future and eyed the machine. It would be so easy to avoid tomorrow and have a do-over. To work together and return to better lives than they ever could've imagined. Maybe if they traveled back two weeks, they could lay more groundwork? They could tell themself not to worry about that fourth strike so they could go straight to the bowling finals. Perhaps if they journeyed to the start of the school year, they could encourage their younger self to pay more attention in math? Or if they went back to fifth grade, they could tell themself to focus on basketball instead of tennis so they could be popular throughout middle school. The possibilities were endless. Why clean up eggshells when you can avoid making a mess in the first place?

Future smiled at Noah. "What do you think? Ready to correct everything wrong with our lives? The two of us planning and working together would be unstoppable. We could orchestrate the perfect universe. No bad days ever again."

Noah blinked, a hazy piece of advice surfacing. "But don't we need the bad days to appreciate the good ones?"

Future frowned. "That sounds like something someone without a time machine would say."

"I just—" Noah picked himself up off the floor. "I'm just

not sure. Mom always says you can't do the same thing over and over and expect a different result."

"You're not listening. We wouldn't do the same things. We would try new things until we got what we wanted. Why aren't you getting this?"

"No, I do. But come on, you've tried nineteen times."

Future shrugged. "You know what they say, the twentieth time is a charm."

"Isn't there something to say about living in the moment?"

"Absolutely. But we can make sure they're the *right* moments."

Noah stared at Future. Perfection was appealing. But as tempting as it was, maybe there was another way. Everyone he cared about—Mom, Dad, Paul, Samar, Darnell—had made it through life without needing a time machine to fix their mistakes. And even though their lives weren't perfect, somehow they managed to move forward and still be fine. Noah pursed his lips. "I just don't think I want to live my life running from and repeating the past. I think…I think you and I have grown apart."

Future winced and wiped his eyes. "Maybe. But deep down we still want the same thing."

"What's that?"

Future shrugged. "The same thing everyone wants. To be good enough."

Noah nodded. "But maybe we're putting too much pressure on ourselves."

"Then take some of that pressure off!" Future said. "Come with me. Let's work together to take control of the universe."

"I think the universe might be too much for a seventh grader to control."

Future shook his head. "Come on, Noah. We can figure this out."

Noah eyed Future. Could they? Should they? He took a deep breath and stuck out a hand. "I'm sorry. I can't."

Future's shoulders deflated. "Really?"

"Really."

Future sighed. "I think you're making a mistake."

"My life has been full of them. So this must mean I'm making the right choice."

The boys' lips curled into smirks.

Future took Noah's hand and shook. "Don't feel sorry for me, okay? Eventually I'm going to make all of this work."

Noah patted Future on the shoulder.

Future nodded and climbed onto the exercise bike. "Well, it's always nice getting to know yourself a little better."

"Take care, Future. Don't feel like you have to run forever, okay?"

Future forced a smile. He leaned forward to the

machine's old laptop, typed a date and time, and hit the *pulse* button on the blender.

He vanished before the blades stopped spinning.

Alone, Noah stared at the empty machine. What now? How could he face his classmates? He could practically hear the insults and feel the cold shoulders. Now and forever, he'd be the kid who got rejected by Lucy Martinez and ripped his pants in front of the whole school. The kid who couldn't wrap his head around Pre-Algebra and would never get into college. Who would never be as good as his older brother. The kid who abandoned and insulted his best friends since the first grade and would have to wander through life by himself. He'd been so close to having everything he thought he wanted, but along the way he'd lost everything he already had. He'd chased perfect, but he only needed his life to be fine. And it used to be. He'd been happy. If only he could get back to that. Maybe he should have gone with Future?

Noah eyed the machine. It was so tempting. Too tempting. He grabbed a screwdriver from his mom's metal toolbox, unscrewed the blender, took it to the kitchen, and made himself a milkshake.

The shake made him feel a little better.

When he finished, he cleaned the counter, collected Future's candy wrappers, and tossed them in the trash.

He felt better still.

Noah went to his room and stared at the clutter. He gathered the rest of the clothes from his floor and began a series of loads of laundry—this time taking care to separate the whites from the colors. He stripped his bed, put on a fresh pair of sheets, dumped the trash from his wastebasket, and picked up the excess garbage that had overflowed from the bin.

Next, he got some spray and cleaned his window, which he and Future had covered with their identical fingerprints.

Finally, Noah got the vacuum from the hall closet and did a slow and orderly pass of his bedroom. Satisfied with the carpet, he got on his belly and peered under his bed. He found three socks, a sweater, and the book on African wildlife he'd checked out from the library three years prior. He vowed to return the book that weekend.

Noah finished cleaning and took a moment to admire the room. He felt 11 percent better about life. Why didn't he clean his room more often?

He sat on his bed, grabbed his guitar, and played. A smile crept across his face.

He became so lost in his playing that he didn't hear his mother come home. When he looked up, she stood in the middle of his room.

"It looks good in here," she said. "You sound great."
Noah blushed.

"I feel like I haven't heard you play in over a week," she continued.

Noah shrugged. "Busy, I guess."

She nodded. "You should try to make time for your talents, sweetie. Especially the ones that make you happy. I don't know where you get it. Everyone else in the family can barely clap in rhythm and you've always been able to pick up an instrument and play. Do you remember when I signed you up for piano when you were five? The teacher said you were wasting your time with kids your age and had you join Paul's private lessons."

Noah tilted his head. "Really? I always thought it was because you wanted Paul and I to spend time together."

"No," she said. "And it's why Paul quit playing piano. He couldn't deal with being so much worse at something than his little brother."

Noah gazed into the carpet. "Huh."

Dr. Nicholson raised an eyebrow and gave a nod. "Dinner will be ready in twenty. You should keep playing."

He smiled and strummed away.

Dr. and Dr. Nicholson were disappointed to hear the election hadn't gone the way Noah hoped, but they were proud of him for putting himself out there. They were more concerned their son had failed a math test. With a handful of advanced mathematics degrees under their belts, they offered to help in any way they could. Noah assured them he could receive tutoring in the afternoons, and that he would start the next day. But first, he would have to go back to school and face his classmates. He couldn't imagine anything more humiliating.

That evening Gourmet May came to an end. Noah's parents finished with a grand finale recipe from a colleague in their physics department: meat loaf.

Noah frowned at the shriveled log while his father cut an endpiece and slid it onto his plate.

"Just try it," his mother said.

Noah cautiously speared a forkful and took a nibble. He surprised himself when he smiled. "It's good."

"Comfort food," proclaimed his father. Noah took another bite. It was exactly what he needed.

Noah reached for a third forkful and heard a key jostle in the lock on the front door. "Paul!"

The Nicholsons jumped from the table and rushed to the living room to find Noah's brother heading down the hall carrying two suitcases with a pillow and a comforter under his arms. Paul's head and shoulders slumped.

"I'm not ready to talk about it," Paul announced. He stepped into his bedroom and shut the door.

Noah's father rubbed his forehead.

"We'll put a plate of meat loaf in the fridge for whenever you're hungry," his mother called.

Noah frowned at his brother's door and at his parents. "Not ready to talk about what?"

His father sighed. "Your brother flunked out of Harvard."

23

TIME TO FACE
THE MUSIC...

The Morning After the Election

On Friday morning, Noah found his brother at the kitchen counter drinking coffee and reading the newspaper. Paul reached over and gave Noah a half hug and a pat on the back. It didn't look like Paul had showered. It didn't smell like it either.

"Sorry about the election," Paul said.

"Sorry about college."

Paul sipped his coffee. "It happens."

"I didn't know you could flunk out of school after only

one bad semester." Noah cringed. "That came out wrong. Sorry. Not trying to hurt your feelings."

Paul shrugged. "They put me on academic probation after my first semester. My second semester sealed it."

Noah's jaw dropped. "Mom and Dad didn't say anything. I had no idea."

"They probably didn't think it was your business."

"Oh. Fair." Noah sized up Paul. He wasn't as big as he remembered. "You gonna be okay?"

"I'll probably mope around the house for a couple months then enroll at the community college. Start over. Just focus on getting good grades for two years so I can transfer to SUNY or the University of Massachusetts."

Noah perked up. "You can do that?"

"You can do that." Paul grimaced at Noah. "Are *you* gonna be okay?"

"I don't know. Not really looking forward to seeing everyone at school."

Paul nodded. "I get it. Need a ride?"

"I guess? Thanks." Noah sighed and closed his eyes. When he opened them they were wet.

"What's wrong?" Paul asked.

"I'm sorry I didn't call you back. I guess I didn't want to talk to you until I did something that you'd be proud of. My whole life I've tried to do everything like you. But you've always had better grades and more friends. I mean, you were captain of the basketball team and I hang out at the bowling alley. I've always wanted to go to Harvard like Mom and Dad. Just like you. But if you couldn't make it work, what chance do I have? And you had it all figured out."

"All figured out?" Paul folded the newspaper and placed it on the counter. "Noah, I've been driving home from school every other weekend to have Mom and Dad do my laundry. And I made some bad choices this year, but that's beside the point. I pushed myself too hard and got burnt out. Everyone has their limit. Look, I love you. You don't have to be perfect for me to be proud. And even though we have things in

237

common, we're different people. So just because I couldn't do something doesn't mean that you can't."

Noah pursed his lips. "Really?"

Paul shrugged. "I guess we'll have to wait and see."

The first person Noah saw outside of school was Claire Trotter. It was hard to miss her in an orange reflective vest directing minivans. Something was different about the front of East Hills. What was it? Oh! The drop-off line wasn't congested with traffic. And all the buses seemed to have been diverted to the campus's side entrance.

Claire waved. "Hi, Noah!"

Noah twisted his lips and waved back. Was she genuinely happy to see him? Weird. Claire blew a whistle at a station wagon and gestured for it to pull forward.

Noah took a deep breath and climbed the school's front steps. It was hard to guess whether the teasing or the shunning would be worse. There was nothing to look forward to and everything to dread. Maybe he should just run home and reattach the blender to the bathtub?

He scowled at the school's door handle, not ready to walk in and face the taunts and looks of pity.

A hand reached past him and opened the door. "Morning,

Noah," Zuri said. She wore her *Lady Leprechauns Dance Team* T-shirt. "Sorry about the election. Plans this weekend?"

Noah stared at Zuri. "What?"

"Do you have plans this weekend?" Zuri asked. "Gregg and I are getting people together to play flag football at Beaman Park."

Noah squinted at Zuri. "You want to hang out this weekend?"

She laughed. "Why wouldn't I? We're friends, right?" She nodded at the open door. "You going to school today?"

"Oh. Thanks." Noah wandered into the crowded building, mystified. Why was Zuri still being nice to him?

A couple of eighth graders bumped into Noah in the hall. "Sorry, Noah," said one. "Bummer about the election," said the other. Noah folded his lips over his teeth, tilted his head, and tried to make sense of it.

Zuri smiled at Noah. "You okay?"

"I'm not really sure."

Down the hall Gregg and Perry grabbed books from their lockers. Noah deflated—obviously they'd clear things up for Zuri and explain he'd become a social outcast. Once a geek, always a geek. But instead, Gregg's face lit up when he saw them.

"Morning, Zuri!" Gregg called. "You ask Noah about the park this weekend?"

"Yeah," she said. "But he hasn't given me an answer."

"You have to come, Noah," Perry said.

"Yeah, everyone is going." Gregg shut his locker. "My mom can probably pick you up if you need a ride. You live on Prescott Drive, right?"

"Uh, yeah," Noah said.

"Cool," Gregg said. "We'll be by around noon. See you in Science."

Gregg and Perry disappeared down the hallway and Zuri hurried after. "See you later, Noah!"

What was happening? His eyes lit up. Future must have rewritten history somehow!

Zuri looked over her shoulder. "Sorry about your pants yesterday! Hopefully you can laugh about it soon!"

Noah frowned. Well, clearly Future hadn't changed a thing. People simply weren't as concerned with the events of the previous day as he was.

But why?

First period was eerily ordinary. No one snickered at Noah. Or teased him. Or seemed to make a joke behind his back. Everyone just nodded, or said "hello," or some version of "tough break yesterday." Mr. Jones rambled on about pollinating flowers and Noah wondered when Mrs. Jones would remind her husband to shampoo his dusty toupee.

Second period began similarly. Pleasant greetings and polite condolences. Noah's Social Studies teacher, Ms. Estrada, compared and contrasted their federal and state governments.

Noah's eyes drifted to the seat closest to the door and his muscles clenched. Katie Frankel slouched at her desk. And guilt flooded in. Noah watched Katie's eyes nervously dart from her notebook to Ms. Estrada, to the left of the room and the right. Her feet swung from her chair, not quite reaching the floor. Then, Katie turned to Noah and held his gaze. He raised a hand and waved. She frowned and looked back to her notes.

When the bell rang, she grabbed her binder and was the first out the door. Noah scooped up his things and bolted after her.

"Katie!"

Her ponytail bounced down the busy hall.

Noah picked up his pace and exchanged smiles and nods with other classmates while he went. "Katie!"

She stopped but didn't turn. He caught up to her and finished shoving his notebook into his bag.

Katie eyed the floor. "What do you want, Noah?"

"I feel bad about the joke I made. It wasn't cool. I shouldn't have said it and I'm sorry."

Katie nodded to the floor. "I was really excited when I heard you were running for president," she told her shoes. "I always thought you were one of the nice ones."

"I am," Noah said with two hands. "Or was? Or at least I want to be again."

She looked up. "Good. I'm sorry you didn't win. I helped tally the results yesterday. I can't believe you lost by one vote. I felt kind of guilty."

Noah took a step back. "I lost by *one* vote?"

"Yep." Katie pushed her slipping glasses up the bridge of her nose. "I don't really know Claire that well, and I wasn't sure if you and me were friends anymore, so I ended up not voting. I guess you losing isn't totally my fault. If I voted for you, we would've had to do a revote because you and Claire would have tied."

Noah closed his eyes and exhaled. "I left school during the assembly and didn't vote either."

"Oh. Yeah, well, I suppose if both of us had voted it would've mattered." Katie patted him on the forearm. "Thanks for saying something about the joke. It was really bothering me. I'm glad we're friends again."

Noah watched as she turned and scurried down the hall, and he wondered what might've been.

24

A WORLD OF POSSIBILITIES...

Twenty-One Hours After the Election

Ms. Tucker wasn't at her desk when Noah walked through her door, but Lucy was at hers. He blushed when he saw her. She looked to her math book when she saw him. Noah sighed and slid into a seat.

Darnell and Samar strolled into class mid-conversation—something about a movie Samar had watched with his parents the night before. The boys stopped talking when they saw Noah. Were they wrestling with whether to take the two empty spots next to him?

Samar stepped toward a couple of seats on the far side of the room and Noah's heart sank, but his determination to fix things didn't. "I've been a jerk lately."

Samar froze. Darnell tilted his head.

"I miss you guys," Noah continued. "Sorry I was selfish and so caught up in the election."

The words dangled in the classroom. Samar and Darnell appeared unmoved. Noah bit his lip—would Future have been impressed by the apology?

"Sorry you lost," Samar said.

"Yeah," Darnell said. "We voted for you."

Noah's eyes went wide. "Really? Thanks."

"Of course," Samar said. "Who else would we vote for?"

Noah smiled. Maybe he wouldn't have to go through the rest of his life without the two of them. "So what have you guys been up to?"

Samar shrugged. "Mostly just practicing for next season at Bowl-O-Rama."

Noah winced. "Sorry again about that. I really did blow it for us twice."

"Yep," Samar said. "But now we'll be more motivated than ever to win it all next year."

"We're going to get a lane tomorrow around lunch," Darnell said. "You should join us."

Noah smiled at Darnell—he was growing more confident

by the day. His comments weren't sounding like questions anymore. Somehow he seemed taller, too.

"Noah's playing flag football at the park with me," Gregg said.

"Maybe we can play football next weekend?" Noah said to Gregg.

Gregg's forehead wrinkled. "Um. Yeah, maybe."

Darnell and Samar took the seats next to Noah, and Gregg sat with the basketball team. Noah looked between the groups. Would he ever be invited to another game at the park again? Maybe it didn't matter. He missed bowling with his friends.

Ms. Tucker hurried through the door just as the bell rang for third period to begin. "Lost track of time grading papers in the teachers' lounge," she announced to the room. "Most of you did very well. Noah, do you think I can see you after class?"

Noah swallowed. "I was thinking I could stop by after school for some extra help."

Ms. Tucker nodded. "I think that's a better idea."

After the final bell, Noah caught up with Samar and Darnell and then headed back toward Ms. Tucker's. While most of the day had turned out better than he expected, his stomach was in knots thinking about that test. What would he even do next year without being in the honors program with his friends? He was so caught up in his worries that he didn't notice Lucy in the empty hallway. He jumped when she closed her locker.

"I saw that," she said. "Don't worry, I'm not going to hit you in the nose again."

He chuckled. "Just startled me a bit."

"Sorry about yesterday," she said.

"You don't have to be sorry," he said. "You shouldn't have to go to a dance with me if you don't want to."

"I know," she said. "I meant sorry about the election."

"Right." Noah took a breath of courage. "Look, I know you don't owe me an explanation, but why didn't you want to go with me? I thought you...well, kind of liked me?"

"I did," she said with a shrug. "But I think that's when I thought you were someone else."

He scratched the back of his head. "What do you mean?"

"Someone who wasn't obsessed with what Gregg and his friends thought. Someone who didn't care whether it was cool to be on a bowling team. Someone who wouldn't insult Katie Frankel to get a laugh—"

"I apologized to her this morning."

"You should have. Someone who didn't care that the

other kids thought it was weird that he dressed like an accountant every day."

Noah frowned at his outfit. "People think my clothes are weird?"

She rolled her eyes. "I used to think that you were someone who was constantly lost in his head worrying about who-knows-what. But also someone who didn't care whether what they did or said made him look or sound like a geek."

Noah considered that last part. "But that *is* who I am."

Lucy smiled. "Well, maybe over time you can prove it to me."

"I'd like to try."

Noah entered Ms. Tucker's classroom and was surprised to find Claire Trotter at a desk in the front row. "Shouldn't you be directing traffic?"

Claire laughed. "Principal Thompson agreed to take over for me in the afternoons."

"Seems like you came up with a good system," Noah admitted.

"Thanks," she said. "I got so tired of seeing everyone stuck in the drop-off line. I reached a breaking point this week after my mom got boxed in again when she was already late for work. I'd been thinking about it for months and figured there had to be a better way."

Noah nodded and took a seat next to her. "Where's Ms. Tucker?"

"She'll be right back. She went to grab a tea for herself and a couple hot chocolates. You like hot chocolate, right? We figured you did."

"A hot chocolate sounds perfect," he said. And it really did. "You're getting tutoring, too? Aren't you taking Algebra with the eighth graders?"

"I'm the tutor."

Noah's face fell. "I thought Ms. Tucker did that."

"She does, too. But I thought a student-to-student tutoring program could be a nice alternative for everyone. It's one of the reasons I ran for president. I'm so thrilled they let me implement my policies right away." Claire smiled. "What would you have done if you won?"

Noah frowned. "I'm still not really sure."

"Huh," she said.

Noah shrugged. "I guess it's good that you're president." And he meant it.

She bit her lip. "You're a good guy, Noah. I've been thinking I could use you in my cabinet. Maybe as treasurer? What do you say?"

Noah smiled and the thought gave him goosebumps. But his smile faded and the tingling stopped. "I say it's a nice offer, but honestly? I think I've been trying to do too much at once. Also, you should probably have someone better at math be your treasurer, so you don't have to constantly double-check their work."

"Fair enough," she said. "What are you going to do with yourself now that you're out of politics?"

"I wish I knew," he said. His knee bounced beneath the desk.

By the time Noah finished talking to Claire, he knew what a variable was and could explain the order of operations, two terms he'd often heard in math class but always figured he'd learn later.

Noah thanked Claire for her time, and she slipped out to enjoy the weekend. He sat with Ms. Tucker and drank the last of his hot chocolate.

"I think you should retake the test after school on Monday," she said.

Noah's face lit up. "I still have a chance to get a B?"

"No," she said. "That wouldn't be fair to your classmates. I have to deduct two letter grades from your score because you bailed on the exam yesterday. But a C or a D is better than a zero."

Noah dropped his head to his hands. "But if I get a C, I won't be in honors next year."

"That's true," she said. "Unless you take summer school."

"Summer school?" Could anything be worse?

Ms. Tucker shrugged. "I guess you'll have to decide what's important to you."

"Honors is hugely important. At least I think." Noah sighed. "I don't really know anymore. I've been through a lot recently. Things have been terrible, and stressful, and a little bit wonderful right before becoming completely embarrassing. It's all been…just really hard."

"Welcome to middle school." Ms. Tucker leaned back in her chair. "I've got good news and bad news. Most of the time what's huge and important and wonderful or terrible and traumatic to one person isn't that big of a deal to everyone else. So you're the one who ultimately needs to decide what matters to you. Other people will be too busy navigating their *own* ups and downs. Maybe that makes us all a little selfish, but we're only human.

"In your life, you're going to have successes and failures and surprises—all kinds of unexpected bumps along the way. And eventually you'll forget ninety-nine percent of them, even though all of that stuff, big and small, shapes who you are. The good *and* the bad. So if staying in honors is that important to you, sign up for summer school and retake Pre-Algebra. Or don't. Have fun this summer and recharge for next year."

Noah's head spun as he grappled with the possibilities.

Ms. Tucker took a sip of tea, leaned forward at her desk, and whispered, "But are you ready to hear the most important thing?"

"Yeah."

"Either way, you're going to be fine."

25

SEEING EYE TO EYE...

Five Minutes Later

Noah walked out of school with a spring in his step. He took a deep breath at the top of the stairs. Had afternoon air ever smelled so good? And had he ever felt so calm? It was like life had provided a restart. He couldn't wait to discover what lay ahead.

Then, he spotted his father's vintage station wagon parked at the curb and his family leaning against the car. He scrunched up his face. What were they doing at school?

"We had a hunch you'd be up for getting milkshakes," his mother called.

"Family and desserts aren't only for celebrating, bucko," his father said. "They're pretty effective at consoling, too. And you've been working hard. You deserve it."

Noah sighed and headed down the steps. "You don't have to hold my hand for *everything*."

His mother frowned. "Hold your hand?"

"Yeah," Noah said. "You're always looking over my shoulder to make sure I'm okay."

His father squinted. "We're your family."

His mother shrugged. "It's kind of in the job description, honey."

"We look out for each other," Paul said.

Noah rolled his eyes. "You don't get it, Paul. Mom and Dad always gave you space. Ever since you left, they've constantly been hovering over me. I mean, they don't even let me use *an iron* in my room."

His father's brow furrowed. "This is about the iron?"

Noah shook his head. "It's not about the iron. I just wish you'd trust me."

"We do trust you," his mother said.

Noah crossed his arms and eyed the sidewalk. "I mean like you trusted Paul when he was my age. You always let him do whatever he wanted."

"Paul?" His mother laughed. "Noah, I don't think we could've paid your brother to make a real decision on his own before he went off to college. And even after that, he called us at least four or five times a day. And he's certainly never used an iron in his life."

"It's true," Paul said. "And I have no regrets about all the time I've saved by living with wrinkles."

Noah tilted his head at his brother. Had Paul's clothes always been so rumpled?

His father grinned and shook his head. "Noah, *you've* always been the independent one. You're so self-reliant that, more often than not, we have to pry things out of you to find opportunities to give advice and make us feel like decent parents."

Noah frowned. "Really?"

"*Really*," his mother said.

"Yeah, Noah," Paul said. "When we were growing up, I felt like I was always the only one talking and asking questions at dinner because you never wanted to share anything."

"Huh," Noah said. Maybe he'd been looking at things all wrong.

"So what do you say?" Paul asked. "Milkshake?"

Noah's eyebrows raised, taken aback by the hope he heard in his brother's voice and saw in his parents' eyes. Just because his family kept an eye on him, didn't mean they didn't trust him. They cared and wanted him to be happy. Just like always. And that felt more than a little bit wonderful.

Noah lifted his chin. "That sounds perfect," he said. "And maybe I can tell you how today ended up being, well, not too bad."

His mother smiled. "We'd love to hear all about that."

Noah exchanged slaps on the back with Paul, hugs with his parents, and climbed into the back seat of the car. As he clicked in the seat belt, something caught his eye outside the window. He stared across the street.

Was that a *butterfly*?

Noah's lips curled into a smirk.

ACKNOWLEDGMENTS

This book was edited by the legendary Alexandra Hightower. I can't imagine having a more brilliant collaborator. Enormous thanks to Megan Tingley, Alvina Ling, and everyone at Little, Brown Books for Young Readers. Special thanks to Mercè López, Jenny Kimura, Crystal Castro, Victoria Stapleton, Esther Reisberg, Marisa Russell, Sadie Trombetta, Emilie Polster, Mara Brashem, Alice Gelber, and Christie Michel.

I am represented by the amazing Janine Kamouh. Endless thanks to Janine and the terrific people at WME, especially James Munro, Alicia Everett, Danny Greenberg, Olivia Burgher, Gaby Caballero, Sabrina Taitz, and Laura Bonner.

I come from a family of bighearted, supportive storytellers. I've found it helpful.

Loads of appreciation to Andy Kimble, Clara Hoffmann, Evie Hoffmann, and Steve Nuchols for early reads and helpful notes. A big thank-you to Dr. Stephon Alexander, professor of physics at Brown University, who I am certain could build a time machine (if he ever found the time).

Thanks to my friends Jordan Hoffmann, Adam Levy, Toby Halbrooks, David Lowery, Ava DuVernay, Jonathan Auxier, Elizabeth Ingold, and Brad Montague for their encouragement and inspiration.

A huge thank-you to all the teachers and librarians working tirelessly to make the world better.

But most of all, thank you to my wife, Erin Malone. If I had the ability to do things over again in life, there are some things I might do differently, but I'd fall in love with her every time.

Erin Borba

ADAM BORBA is also the author of *Out-side Nowhere* and *The Midnight Brigade*. When he's not writing, he develops and produces movies like *Pete's Dragon* and *Peter Pan & Wendy* with his friends. He is a graduate of Palm Springs High School, the University of Southern California, and the William Morris Agency mailroom. *This Again?* is his third novel. Adam lives in California with his family. He invites you to visit him online and inquire about school or library visits at adamborba.com.

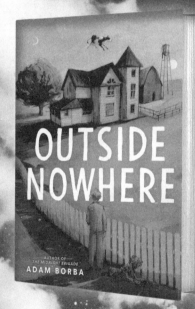